A MAGICAL ALLIANCE

A MAGICAL ALLIANCE

MAGIC CITY CHRONICLES™ BOOK TWO

TR CAMERON   MICHAEL ANDERLE   MARTHA CARR

DISRUPTIVE IMAGINATION

Copyright © 2021 LMBPN Publishing
Cover by Fantasy Book Design
Cover copyright © LMBPN Publishing
A Michael Anderle Production

LMBPN Publishing
PMB 196, 2540 South Maryland Pkwy
Las Vegas, NV 89109

First US edition, February, 2021
ebook ISBN: 978-1-64971-437-4
Print ISBN: 978-1-64971-438-1

THE A MAGICAL ALLIANCE TEAM

Thanks to the JIT Readers

Dave Hicks
Peter Manis
Daniel Weigert
John Ashmore
Dorothy Lloyd
Wendy L Bonell
Paul Westma
Angel LaVey
Larry Omans
Kelly O'Donnell

If I've missed anyone, please let me know!

Editor
Skyhunter Editing Team

For those who seek wonder around every corner and in
each turning page. And, as always, for Dylan.

— TR Cameron

To Family, Friends and
Those Who Love
To Read.
May We All Enjoy Grace
To Live The Life We Are
Called.

— Michael

CHAPTER ONE

Ruby stumbled backward with a bellow of pain from the blow that slammed into her ribs. "Damn, ow, damn, bloody gods damned." She bit down on the inappropriate name she was about to call her mentor, but Keshalla's grin suggested that even unspoken, she'd nonetheless communicated it.

The other woman wielded paired swords for the test. The Mist Elves' combat arts required students to demonstrate mastery of each weapon before being permitted to begin their study of the next. Her teacher had deemed her ready to display her skills with a single sword. She had no doubts at the start of the process, but as it wore on, her confidence was starting to flag. *It's okay, Ruby. It'll only be another year of training if you fail.* Her stomach clenched at the prospect of facing her mentor's disappointment for that long.

The ritual involved rounds of combat against each style of weapon, meaning she'd faced children who had mastered the earliest ones, generally projectiles, at the start. Now, after almost an hour of defending herself from ranged weapons and defeating opponents using melee ones, she was up against one of the most skilled warriors her people had to offer. And she was losing. In front of an audience made up of the entire village, who ringed the central grassy area between their small houses that was her frequent training ground on Oriceran.

The stakes got progressively higher as one advanced. She'd taken body hits from sling stones, had several cuts on her face and hands from arrows and thrown blades, and had been battered by force-shielded knives, bladed sticks, and swords. At first, the goal was not to get hit too much. Now it was all about staying up long enough to defeat her opponent, which was unlikely against Keshalla, or until her mentor deemed her worthy, which Ruby thought was still within her reach. *Okay. Focus. Do this.*

Ruby set her feet and ran the back of her bare hand over her forehead to get stray wisps of white-blonde hair out of her eyes. The small trickle of magic she applied to cover the edge of her single sword was no more draining than the power she used on Earth to maintain the illusion of her humanity. Other magic was prohibited, although she had been given sufficient cause during the bouts to wonder if that was true for her opponents as well. She'd never been on the opposite side of the test and was confident that many of her foes were powerful enough to hide their use of magic if they chose to.

She charged her teacher, who hadn't pursued her retreat. Keshalla stood an inch or two taller than Ruby, giving her a slight advantage in reach. Her pale skin would show cuts as easily as Ruby's—*if anyone ever managed to strike her*—but their appearances diverged from there. The other woman's shining black hair, a rarity among the Mist Elves, whipped around as she spun out of the way. Ruby's sword almost caught the black and crimson leather armor, another rare choice divergent from the traditional nature colors their people preferred.

Ruby instinctively flicked her sword up to block the counterattack, intercepting a blade on its way to her head as she spun to disengage. She felt the tip of the second sword as it scraped across her thigh, but her move neutralized the power behind it. The other woman's grin showed her pleasure in the fight, and hopefully in her student. However, it failed to completely conceal the strategist's smile—the expression of the opponent who was clearly trying to wear her down, to use the effort she'd put into the previous bouts against her.

Ruby brought her sword up to high guard position in a two-handed grip, pommel above her head, blade angled downward. "What do you say we call this done and go have a drink?"

Keshalla spun her swords in a flashy display, then set her stance with one held before her in defense, the other at eye level pointing forward. "I would never dishonor you in that way. You've come so far, *minari*. Your victory is at hand." Her tone was equal parts encouraging and mocking.

"Sure, *shenai*. I can tell you're almost ready to give up." At the other woman's laugh, she charged. She moved to her right and cut back across her body, an awkward move that avoided her foe's attempt to block it. A moment of hope turned into frustration as her teacher snapped up a kick that hit the flat of the blade and knocked it out of line.

Two can play at that game. Ruby dropped into a crouch and tried for a foot sweep, knowing Keshalla would probably be able to evade it. *How she'll do it, that's the question.* When the other woman leapt into the air, it was the choice of her teacher, not the warrior, since it created a vulnerability. Ruby exploded upward and smashed into her foe, knocking the defensive blade out of the way with hers, and carried her down to the ground. She made sure to fall hard on her opponent, hoping to knock the breath out of her.

She landed on a force shield. "Not fair," she growled as she rolled to the side and came up in a defensive crouch.

Keshalla rose and nodded. "No one promised it would be."

The sound of tearing grass caused her to snap her head to the left. It took a moment to process the sight of one of the car-sized boulders flying through the air at her. She dove out of the way as it sped through the spot she'd just occupied, *mostly* sure it wouldn't have fatally damaged her if her evasion had been too slow. Her teacher was choosy about the students she taught and killing one outright seemed like a bad signal to send future recruits.

It was a clear message that Ruby needed to get on with it. She charged again, whirling her blade around in a slash at the other woman's head. Both swords came up to block, and she delivered a front kick to her teacher's sternum, knocking her backward. A low cut brought one of the defending blades down, and she stabbed forward at Keshalla's chest. Her foe spun away, but Ruby was ready for it. She dashed ahead and released the sword with her right hand, slashing at the twirling form with her left. That attack was blocked, but the punch connected. It hit the other woman's shoulder rather than her intended strike on the chest but still put her off balance for an instant.

Ruby slipped forward and blasted a knee into the other woman's stomach. She was forced onto the defensive as the twin swords licked out at her face, her chest, then her legs, moving her weapon in a series of slashes and circles to block. When the flurry ended, she resumed the pressure, stepping in close and stabbing at her opponent's thigh. When the blades came down in defense, Ruby snapped her head forward in a strike at Keshalla's nose.

It never landed. Instead, the pommel of one of her foe's swords smashed into her face, bloodying her nose and possibly fracturing her cheek, based on the blast of pain that accompanied it. She blindly swiped a circle with her sword, and a *clang* that almost knocked the weapon from her hand rewarded her as she intercepted a slash at her already aching ribs. Fearing where the other blade was and still unable to see from the tears inspired by the damage to her face, she ran forward with her weapon held at guard before her, hoping to either slam into her opponent or get clear.

The move apparently caught Keshalla by surprise, maybe because it was more aggressive than Ruby tended to be. Regardless, she dashed the tears from her eyes as she reset her stance and faced her opponent. Respect was visible in her teacher's expression, and the other woman nodded as she stepped back into a defensive posture.

Ruby advanced, weaving her sword slowly in a figure-eight before her, keeping her vision soft so the other woman's entire body received equal attention. Watching the eyes or the hands was a great way to get stabbed; it was usually the core and the legs that revealed an opponent's intentions. When she reached the outer circle of engagement, that distance where a quick step and an extended thrust could reach flesh, Keshalla's weight moved slightly onto her front leg. Ruby whirled in a crouching spin to her right as her foe exploded forward, both blades barely missing. She continued the movement with a slash at her foe's legs that connected with a thigh, staggering the other woman.

Keshalla twisted and brought the nearer blade around in another slam at Ruby's damaged side. She accepted the blow and screamed as the pain in her ribs doubled. The fact that she could still breathe indicated that the leather armor, reinforced in that spot, had again kept the fragile bones from breaking. She punched forward with the hilt of her sword, striking her teacher in the left shoulder, dislocating the joint. The blade on that side fell from numbed fingers, and Ruby circled in that direction.

What might have taken a lesser opponent out of the fight was nothing more than a challenge to her mentor. The single remaining sword whipped in, curving over her block to seek her injured cheek. Ruby leaned back to avoid it, then fell as the other woman flipped the weapon in her grip and made the same cut in reverse. She rolled into a backward somersault and came up running at her foe.

She swung her sword high, forcing Keshalla to block it, then delivered a roundhouse kick to the wounded arm. Her teacher gasped, unable to ignore that extra pain. Ruby planted her kicking foot and threw herself into a spin parallel to the ground, one foot slamming the other woman in the chest while the other kicked at the back of her legs. The takedown worked, and she whipped the blade of her sword into position at her teacher's throat.

Keshalla grinned. "Well done, *minari*. Only one step remains."

For a moment, Ruby relaxed, thinking her teacher meant the announcement that she'd passed the test. A feral growl from the other side of the clearing revealed that it was nothing of the sort. She sighed. "You all suck."

Keshalla laughed. "Surely you didn't think your challenge would be the same as one who had not undergone the *venamisha*."

"You know, I kind of did."

"Hopefully after today, you'll be smarter. You may use every power at your disposal. The fight ends when one surrenders or cannot continue."

Ruby rose and turned toward the giant tiger at the other end of the grassy field, half again as large as any Earth had ever produced. "All right, kitty. Bring it on."

CHAPTER TWO

Idryll, the shapeshifting cat-woman who considered herself bound for life to Ruby, charged with another roar. She was gorgeous in this form, her coloring similar to an Earth tiger's, but in shades that had never exactly been present on that planet. They seemed to morph and blend as she advanced, the muscles' movement under that fur almost frightening in their smoothness. Her mouth oddly twisted as she spoke, and as always it was weird hearing speech out of her fully feline form. "You didn't think I'd miss out on the fun, did you?"

Ruby gave a small shrug. "Again, it appears I kind of did. From here on out, I'll assume that you'll complicate everything."

The tiger chuffed a laugh. "Good plan." She surged forward, covering the space between them in seconds. Fortunately, Ruby was ready for it. She wrapped a shield of force magic around her left arm from elbow to fingertips and used it to intercept her foe's slashing claws as she darted to the side to avoid getting run over. She flicked out her sword at Idryll, but her opponent dropped and rolled away, dodging it easily.

They circled one another. Ruby moved carefully to keep her balance centered while her opponent bounced from spot to spot, feigning attacks. When they drew a response, the tiger got that smile that perfectly communicated mockery. Ruby bit down on a sarcastic comment, knowing it would feed her rival's poor attitude. *The next time she falls asleep in normal cat form, I'm throwing her in a bathtub full of cold water.* It was tough to reconcile the killer in front of her with the purring furball that filled her sister Morrigan with delight.

She pulled back the shield from her hand and sent a bolt of frost at her opponent. Idryll scrambled out of the way, but Ruby kept firing, ensuring that the cat stayed on the run. *Just a little more.* Finally, the position was perfect, and she lunged with her sword, shoving it into the path of her foe's paws. The tiger tripped, going over in a somersault. That was the good part.

There were two bad parts. The first was that Idryll's momentum ripped the sword out of her hand and sent it flying. The second was that, when her opponent came up from the ground, she was still smiling. She growled, "Aww. You lost your pointy stick." A wide smile displayed clean white fangs as if to reinforce the resulting imbalance in their fighting tools.

Ruby focused her magic into a force shield that covered her from toes to fingertips. If she was honest with herself, she preferred hand-to-hand combat; it was more visceral, more rewarding, than operating at a distance. *Maybe not against a tiger five or six times my weight.* She didn't doubt that the tiger's move to circle away from the fallen weapon was an invitation to a trap, one that she wasn't about to step into.

The key would be to stay fast and nimble and avoid any situation where Idryll could bring her weight to bear. Although the force shield would protect her from being crushed, for a while anyway, her mentor would chalk it up as a defeat. *I am* so *not going through this again, so I better not fail.*

She ran straight at her rival, and the tiger jumped to meet her. Ruby slid underneath and snapped a kick upward that caught the cat in the air. It didn't have much on it but still made her feel that she'd accomplished something useful. Doubtless her partner underestimated Ruby's unarmed combat skills, so it was a good moment to disabuse her of that notion and maybe take some of her foe's most extravagant and risky attacks off the table.

They rose simultaneously, and the tiger prowled toward her, body low to the ground, tail twitching. The growls coming from deep within Idryll's chest would have been terrifying if it had been a real battle. Knowing it wasn't didn't eliminate the fear entirely, and Ruby forced herself to relax. When the attack came, it was a quick leap forward and the swipe of a massive paw at her legs.

She leapt over the sweep and blocked the expected counterattack from the other paw with a downward swing of her arm. The instant her boots hit the ground, she snapped out a sidekick at her foe and struck the tiger in the shoulder. It was like attacking a wall, and instead of sending her opponent flying, as it would have done to a human, the blow pushed Ruby backward. She stumbled and caught herself, but not in time to escape the tiger's rush.

Idryll slammed into her, throwing her onto her back. The impact sent a wave of agony through her damaged face, followed by a moment of terror as the huge body blotted out the sun as it arced above her. She rolled to avoid being smashed, but a paw caught her with a glancing blow on her ribs before she could get clear. She shouted in pain, hurting her face more, and bounced up filled with anger and adrenaline.

Her opponent was as keen to mix it up as she was, and they met in a clash of bodies. Ruby reinforced the shield on her left arm and used it to bash her way in close, then punched with her right, two fast jabs and an uppercut. The finishing move would have struck true, but the tiger turned into Idryll's cat-woman form without any visible transition. Her body was that of a Mist Elf but covered in fur except for her face, which was bare. Her eyes were still a cat's eyes, and her long hair flowed in the same colors the tiger had worn.

Ruby spat a curse and lunged for her, but the other woman spun away with a laugh. This form was slower than the tiger but still faster than she was. The spin turned into a kick, and she ducked under the heel that sought her temple and the follow-up roundhouse kick that tried for her damaged ribs again.

This version of her partner wasn't nearly as difficult to tackle though, and Ruby drove into her bodily, taking her down to the ground. The other woman shifted her body to make sure she landed on top, but the force shield took the brunt of the impact. Then it was all knees, elbows, and foreheads as they sought an advantage. Ruby took a shot to the temple that scattered stars across her vision but saw through them to get her foe in an armbar. She wrenched herself to the side for leverage, then pressed the joint down, threatening to break the elbow. Idryll shouted, "I yield," and the fight was over.

Ruby collapsed off her, wheezing. Exhaustion washed over her for a moment, then passed, leaving her tired and sore but functional. A groan escaped as she climbed to her feet, and she gave an annoyed snarl at her partner when she bounced up as if they hadn't been fighting. "You suck. By that, I mean that you suck more than anyone in the past has ever sucked. You've reached new and amazing heights of suckage. Or lows. Whichever it is."

The cat-woman laughed and busied herself brushing the dirt and dust from her fur. "Please. I am the very model of restraint. You still have all your limbs."

The truth of it was that the tiger form could probably have done significant damage, even through her shields. She didn't have a read yet on the magic the shapeshifter possessed, and Idryll had rebuffed several questions about it. *One day I'll figure you out.* She turned to face the other woman of mystery in her life as Keshalla walked up to them. "So, did I succeed?"

Her teacher nodded. "Yes. Once you retrieve your sword, you can clean it completely and thoroughly as a penalty for letting yourself be disarmed. Then, you can polish it, after which you whet it. Once that is done, you may sheath it and consider yourself adequate with the single blade. Then, you can take a healing potion to fix your face."

Idryll commented, "Nothing can fix her face."

Ruby stuck her tongue out at the cat before turning her attention back to her mentor. "Then I guess we'll be starting with paired blades soon."

Keshalla shrugged. "Perhaps. From what I saw today, you might need a refresher in unarmed combat."

Ruby scowled. "I was fighting a *tiger*."

"If you're lucky that's the worst thing you'll ever face. One would be a fool to rely on luck."

There was no arguing. She gave a small bow. "Yes, *shenai*." Turning to her partner, she said, "I better get to it. I'm in desperate need of a bath, some aspirin, and a nap, hopefully in that order."

The cat-woman's laugh held both happiness and mockery. "You certainly are. I would hope not to have to fight hand-to-hand again with someone who smells as bad as you do anytime soon."

Ruby clamped her lips shut, knowing that any reply would serve as a reward to Idryll. *I'll get you, kitty cat. I don't know when, I don't know how, but it will happen. And it will be glorious.*

CHAPTER THREE

Ruby sank into the oversized tub with a grateful sigh, her tired muscles getting the reward she'd promised them for hours. Setting her sword to rights and finishing up the other tasks Keshalla had assigned her hadn't taken a ridiculous amount of time, but she had spent every minute of it imagining what this bath would feel like. It had only required five minutes after portaling home for her to draw the water, stash her sword, and get undressed. Now, with the liquid lapping up to her cheeks and the rest of her body submerged beneath a mountain of moisturizing bubbles, she finally felt a glow of accomplishment for successfully passing the test.

The sound of the door opening didn't startle her. She'd locked the outer door to her room, so it could only be one person. She'd concluded that trying to preserve modesty where her shapeshifting life-partner was concerned simply wasn't worth the effort. Idryll sat on the edge of the tub. "Better?"

Ruby closed her eyes again. "Definitely better." It felt

even more relaxing than the healing potion had, which was saying something.

She felt and heard Idryll swishing the water with her hand and smiled inwardly at what she thought of as cat-like behavior. The other woman observed, "You did well, all things considered."

"I'm sure there are many lessons I should take from the experience, and I'm equally sure that Keshalla will share them with me. Repeatedly. Intensively."

Her partner laughed. "That does sound like something she'd do."

Ruby adjusted her position to get as much of her head as possible underwater while still being able to breathe. "It's been quite a frenzy the last few days, with the test coming right on the heels of the kidnapping. If there'd been any chance of a positive response, I would have asked for some time off in between."

"Speaking of which, we're not planning to let the criminals get away with that, are we?"

Ruby shook her head, enjoying how her hair floated. "We are not. But we'll need to be careful. They've shown a lack of concern about who they hurt on the way to getting what they want. While you and I can handle that, we'll have to make sure it doesn't blow back on anyone else."

"Disguises, then."

"At a minimum. Maybe it's enough to tell Sheriff Alejo. I don't know. It's something I need to think a little more about."

The other woman's tone was decisive. "We should handle it ourselves. This is *our* place."

"It's also the sheriff's place, and I'm sure she feels as

strongly about the issue. As I said, we'll have to think about it."

Idryll scoffed, "You cannot *think* your problems to death. That's why we have fangs." Ruby opened her eyes to see the other woman's grin displaying her teeth to full effect and laughed.

"Mine aren't nearly as impressive as yours can be." Her stomach growled, loud in the water, and she laughed again. "If there's one thing I need as much as a nap, it's food. Should be dinnertime pretty soon, so I guess I'd better head down."

Idryll nodded. "I like this plan to get food. Be sure to bring me something tasty." Unspoken was the remainder of the sentence, which went something like "If you'd like to keep your arms intact," but the message still came across clearly. "I think I'll take a nap." The tiger-woman wandered out the door, and Ruby climbed out of the bathtub. She wrapped her head in one towel and gathered another around her body, then padded into her bedroom. It was elegant in an understated way, with lots of intricately carved heavy wood furniture.

She grabbed clothes out of her dresser. Since she was planning to stay at the house overnight, she went with yoga pants and an oversized T-shirt, and once her hair was acceptably towel-dried, she pulled it back into a ponytail. She checked her look in the mirror and shook her head. "Not really dressed to impress." It was good enough for family, though. They didn't know about her role in thwarting the kidnapping, of course, but they were aware she'd been on Oriceran for her test, and she always returned from those in need of a rest. As she headed for the door, she passed Idryll, now in the form of a Bengal house cat of unusual size, and petted her before heading out of the room.

Ruby made it halfway down the stairs before spotting Matthias, the employee who more or less ran the house for her parents and who had been a third parent while she and her siblings were growing up. He was still tall and thin and still looked like he might have walked off the set of *The Lord of the Rings*. She broke into a grin and rushed down to hug him. The older man returned both the smile and the embrace and asked, "So, did it go well?"

Ruby nodded. "It was a challenge, of course, but I passed."

The man's grin grew wider. "Fantastic news, Miss Ruby. I'm so glad to hear it. The kitchen has made one of your favorite meals tonight."

She took his arm as he walked her toward the dining room. "Pizza?" He shook his head. "Vegetable lasagna?" He repeated the motion. She smacked him lightly on the hand. "What is it, then?"

He laughed. "You'll have to wait and see."

She scowled. "Traitor." Matthias nodded, seeming unmoved by the insult. "I'll need a dish of meat for the kitty cat upstairs. A lot of it."

"Of course. I'll have it ready for you when dinner is over." Idryll had some inborn magic that allowed her forms to function on whatever meal was appropriate to the shape she possessed at the moment. Her human version would be content as long as her cat form was full. Ruby had rather expected the situation to be more like the superhero The Flash, who had to eat all the time to sustain his metabolism, at least according to the TV show and the movies. "I don't suppose Dralen is out of the house?"

Matthias chuckled. "No such luck. I believe he has a new idea for improving the casino to share."

Ruby groaned. "Improvement is in the eye of the beholder, or something like that." She released his arm and drew a deep breath as they arrived at their destination. "Okay, here I go." She knew her complaints about family amused him and always laid it on thick for his benefit.

She stepped through the doorway to the dining room and found her relatives in their usual positions. Her father Rayar sat at the head of the table, her mother Sinnia on his right with Morrigan beside her, and her brother Dralen at the patriarch's left hand. She took her seat across from her sister and stuck her tongue out at her. Morrigan responded in kind, and their mother rolled her eyes.

Rayar asked, "So, what news?"

"I passed." Her father clapped, her mother beamed, and even Dralen grinned and nodded.

Morrigan congratulated her, adding, "From what I heard, you lost your sword."

Ruby scowled. "I don't know who you've been talking to, brat, but it was a strategic move. Entirely intentional." She managed to hold the stern expression for a few seconds, but her sister's knowing grin broke her restraint. "Yeah, okay, maybe not completely planned. It worked. That's what counts."

"I'll have my test on the bow soon. Maybe you could come to watch." Those who were less advanced couldn't watch those of a higher skill level test unless they were involved in it, and then only until they'd done their part, to prevent them from getting too much information about what awaited them in their training. She imagined Morrigan had probably tried to be one of her opponents during the trial, but tradition would argue against allowing a family member into the mix if anyone else was available. Dralen hadn't taken to the traditional weapons, and their parents had agreed to his request not to train. She was glad her sister hadn't chosen the same path.

"I'll certainly try to be there, assuming Keshalla doesn't have me spend all my time relearning things I didn't do well enough during my test."

Her brother interrupted, "So, after the attack on the Atlanteans, we need to beef up security at Spirits. I thought Ruby could create some detectors that would look for dangerous technological and magical devices, plus any tools players could use to cheat at the tables." He turned toward her as he spoke, and his expression was questioning.

She nodded slowly. "I could modify some existing sensors that do those separately and combine them without too much trouble. Adding in the anti-cheating stuff might be difficult, but if we're willing to pay Margrave's rates, he'll probably agree to work with me on it."

Dralen grinned and turned to face their father. "See? I told you she'd be into it."

Rayar chuckled. "You were right. Truly, it seems like a good idea. The other owners I've talked to all plan to increase their security significantly after what happened at the Mist and the Ebon Dragon."

Ruby asked, "The Council, you mean?"

He shook his head. "No, the Council hasn't met formally about it yet, although obviously we'll be in favor. In our capacity as individual casino owners, it clearly makes sense."

The conversation paused as dinner arrived, big baking dishes full of tamales. Ruby grinned and grabbed the nearest before Morrigan could, shoveling several onto her plate. Her sister said, "I was chatting with a dealer and overheard a guard talking. Not one of the ones on our staff, but one from our security company. He said his employer has been getting pressure to sell out to a bigger firm."

Her mother frowned. "Did he say which one?"

Morrigan shook her head. "No, that was all I heard, and I didn't want to seem like I was eavesdropping."

Ruby interjected, "Although you totally were." It earned her another playful dirty look from her sister, but instead of returning it, she looked at her parents. "Will that change our plans?"

Her mother shrugged. "Perhaps, although these things happen in human businesses all the time, as I understand it. From our perspective, it will probably be invisible. They might not even change the company's name."

Her father looked thoughtful. "Nonetheless, it's worrisome. Competition is a good thing, and if companies merge or combine, our options dwindle. Perhaps I should talk to the Council about creating our own security company, rather than relying on the mostly human businesses around here." To Ruby's knowledge, all but one was human-owned, and that one was human co-owned, although all of them employed magicals to one degree or another since many of the threats they would deal with in Ely were magical.

She let the conversation drop, and talk turned to more normal things: Morrigan's studies and training, Dralen's work on his MBA, her parents' plan to renovate the hotel portion of Spirits, which seemed to be forever under construction in one way or another. As dinner wrapped up, she caught her father's eyes and glanced at the door to the study. He lifted an eyebrow before nodding. The family members all shared hugs, and Ruby declined the offer to play a game with Morrigan since exhaustion already nipped at the edges of her brain. She'd planned to go straight up to bed after the meal but now thought having a chat with her father was important enough to delay that priority a little. *Maybe I can get him to spill some secrets. Worth a try, anyway.*

CHAPTER FOUR

Her father took one of the big comfortable leather chairs, and Ruby sat in the other. Matthias brought them each coffee, and while she worried for a moment that the caffeine might keep her awake, she decided it would have to be pretty amazing to accomplish that feat given how tired she was. He asked, "So, what's up?"

She frowned, wondering how to say it. "You know my roommate Demetrius, right?"

Rayar nodded. "I know of him, although we haven't met. You should invite them all down for dinner at some point."

She waved a hand. "Once things settle down, maybe. He's pretty well tapped into the rumor mill. He told me there's a connection between one of the security companies and the kidnapping."

Her father leaned forward. "Really? How does he know? Which one?"

The intensity of his gaze suggested he was acting in

both of his roles, as the owner of Spirits and as Council member. *Probably as a concerned citizen, as well.* "A place called Aces Security is what he said. I have no idea about the validity of his source. He clearly doesn't want to share that information, and I'm reluctant to ask for fear that he'll be unwilling to tell me other stuff." Keeping her first-hand knowledge of the company secret seemed like a smart move since it would be difficult to explain without revealing things she didn't want anyone to know.

He leaned back in his chair with a frown and sipped from the heavy mug. "That's not good if it's true. Aces is one of the bigger ones, and the rumors *I've* heard say that if acquisitions do thin out the security companies, they're more likely to be buying than be bought."

"Could that give them a reason to be involved in the kidnapping? Maybe trying to make things seem more dangerous? Or putting direct pressure on the Atlanteans? I don't think they provide security for the Kraken."

Her father shook his head. "You're right, and what you say is certainly possible. This is a matter I'll have to share with the Council tonight."

She sipped her coffee again, then set it aside. "Well, I thought it was something you might want to know. Now, it's bedtime."

She stood and stepped forward with a yawn, expecting him to wrap her in a hug. Instead, he rose and held her at arm's length. "I think you should come to the meeting and relate this information first-hand."

She blinked. None of the family other than her father had ever been to a Council meeting, as far as she knew. "Really?"

He nodded. "Really. When I consider the three of you and how my responsibilities will fall out when I'm no longer capable of handling them, I see your brother running the casino's day-to-day operations, your sister being the people person who makes the connections and the partnerships, and you as the politician and strategist. That means the sooner you get to know the Council, the better."

"Wouldn't mother be a stronger choice?" Ruby was a little overwhelmed at being given the big picture so suddenly.

He laughed. "Your mother wants nothing to do with the Council. She's said so many times. We've discussed it, and she agrees you should be the one."

"Even though I'm supposedly a human?"

Her father nodded somberly. "You're in a unique position. You can bring your perspective from that side of things to the Council and still have the authority of being part of the family."

"Do they know that I'm not *really* human?"

He shook his head. "It remains a secret from everyone outside this house."

She sighed. "Of course I'll come. I don't suppose you'd care to tell me why we're continuing to pretend I'm human though, would you?"

Normally she got a joke or brushoff, but this time he simply looked down into her eyes. "I can only say it has to do with keeping you safe. There's an old tale, supposedly from an oracle among the mystics." She snorted, and he laughed with a nod. "Yes, I know. I thought it was pretty hokey early on, too. But it mentioned our family, specifically your mother's bloodline. It talked of a first child, a girl who would be in danger from those seeking to thwart her potential. So once we knew you weren't going to be male, we hid your birth and lied about your age. You're one of the main reasons we first came to this planet, knowing it would be a better place to protect our child if the story turned out to have any truth to it."

She forced herself to close her mouth, which hung open in shock. That was more than she'd ever heard about it. *Reaching the quarter-century mark has indeed been crossing a threshold of some kind.* "Okay. That's awfully mysterious. Is there more you can tell me?"

He gave a small nod. "Only one more thing. The story said that person would undergo the *venamisha*. So, you see, it's even more vital now than ever that we keep you safe, in case you turn out to be the one mentioned in the story, and in case the story turns out to be real."

She shook her head. "Have you seen a doctor lately? I think you might have mental issues."

Her father laughed and pulled her into a hug. "Go take a nap. You'll need to be at your best when we see the Council. Tonight, midnight."

She walked toward the stairs in a haze. *The world has gone crazy, and right now I'm way too tired to deal with its nonsense. Idryll better not be taking up the whole bed, or she'll find herself sleeping on the floor.*

Jared Trenton was not a happy man. The message to go to the airport had come from the boss with no warning at all, only a "Do this now." He'd been in the middle of what had seemed a very promising date but had dutifully made his apologies and immediately jumped into his car for the drive. He couldn't even make calls because this was one of those off-the-books moves that required his phone to be locked in the signal-proof box in his car and the vehicle's location system to be off. It wouldn't have been so bad if it was a short trip, but it was almost two hours from Ely, Nevada to the Elko Regional Airport. He muttered curses along the way: at the man who employed him, at his partner for not successfully finishing the kidnapping of the Atlantean brat, and at all of Magic City in general for refusing to roll over and acquiesce to his desires.

At this time of night, the airport was mostly shut down, but the entrance he'd been told would be open was ready to permit him access. The plane he'd come to meet was already on the tarmac: a nondescript private jet, the kind any business might use. He flashed his headlights in the signal he'd been given. The door opened, portable steps folded down, and a figure was silhouetted briefly in the doorway before it descended the stairs. He hit the button to release the hatch and climbed out, extending a hand to take the man's bag as he drew near. His cargo, a person of Asian descent with light hair, dark eyebrows, sharp cheekbones, and a mouth that turned down in a frown, shook his head slightly and put his duffel into the car. Jared shrugged and slammed the hatch. "Door's open." He circled the driver's side and got behind the wheel.

His passenger entered a moment later and pulled out a pistol, resting it comfortably in his lap with his finger on the guard and the barrel pointed at the vehicle's other occupant. Jared said, "That's unnecessary."

The other man shrugged. "I decide what is necessary for me. In this case, I don't know you, so it is."

Jared smothered a sigh. "Fine. Whatever. I'm Jared. And you are?"

"You may call me Goryo."

"Just that?"

"It's all you need to know."

This is going to be a wonderful trip. He put his foot on the gas and steered out, heading back toward Magic City. "So, anything you can share about why you're in town?"

The other man's flat and uninformative expression remained unchanged. "If our mutual employer wished for you to know, he would have told you. Since he hasn't, I must presume he does not wish you to know. It would be entirely foolish of me to go against his decision."

"Yeah, the boss enjoys being a man of mystery, no doubt about that. But, come on, that doesn't mean we can't work together. If I understand what you're planning, I can help you. My ultimate goal is to see the boss's plans succeed." *And to make a pile of money for myself while cornering the market on security in town.*

Goryo shrugged. "What do you have to offer?"

Jared smiled. "Only the best of everything. Tech, weapons, vehicles, personnel. I have it all, anything you could want. And if you need untraceable people, I can arrange for that too."

"A vehicle would be useful. On the other matters, I am entirely self-sufficient. You can tell me, though, where the pawnshops in town are."

Jared frowned. "Pawnshops? Really?" The other man stared at him. "Yeah, okay. Well, there are a couple of big ones called Lucky's, owned by Lucky Tomasso. That's where most of the gamblers who are looking for a little extra scratch wind up selling family heirlooms to avoid getting their kneecaps broken. Plus about a dozen smaller shops scattered around town, offering more specialized stuff. Some do jewelry, others do antiques, and there's even one that does mainly musical instruments. I can get you a map with all of them on it."

Goryo nodded. "That will be adequate."

"Why do you need a pawnshop?" Jared cursed inwardly at himself. *Not doing a great job of making myself look in control here. Of course, the truth is we're not.* Grentham was deeply annoyed that their boss, Gabriel "The Nightmare" Sloane, was running an operation in their town that didn't include them. Jared had tried to be the voice of reason, but he wasn't at all pleased with it either. It was on the one hand an insult, a suggestion they couldn't handle things on their own. On the other hand, though, they still had tasks to perform for the boss, so at least they weren't being cut out of the loop. *Maybe it requires some specialty we don't possess.* He scowled. *Kidnapping, perhaps.* He jerked his mind back from where it had been wandering. "Sedan or SUV?"

<hr>

The rest of the drive passed in annoying silence. He pulled into the garage at Aces Security, and his passenger stepped out, retrieved his bag, and pointed at another large black sport utility vehicle. "That one will do."

Grentham, who had come out to meet them, angled to the key box on the wall and grabbed the ones for that SUV. He tossed them to their guest, who snatched them cleanly out of the air with economical grace. He marched over to the vehicle, climbed in, and drove off without another word. Jared watched him depart, shook his head, then turned to his partner. "Let's see where he goes." They walked into the security station and ordered the tech on duty to call up the car's tracer on the main monitor. Newly installed screens above it displayed camera views of the building's exterior. They'd bolstered their defenses immediately after being broken into, cameras being the quickest and easiest option.

A moving yellow dot overlaid a map of the area, and after several minutes it slowed to a stop. Jared asked, "What's he doing? Why would he stop in the middle of nowhere?"

The answer came a moment later as the dot disappeared. Grentham, dressed all in black as always with his black mustache and braided beard perfectly styled, grunted. "Guess he doesn't want us to know where he's going."

Jared chuckled. "Secretive bastard. Fine, then. Let's go upstairs and chat." He headed up to his office and sat behind his desk. The dwarf sat opposite him. "So, think this jerk will get in our way?"

His partner shrugged. "If he does, we'll have to arrange for him to have an accident. I'm all for letting the boss make our lives easier, but we're certainly not giving up any of our hard-won territory to some asshole outsider."

Jared nodded thoughtfully. "I can't imagine he's here for the same reason we are, though. Seems like it must be something special the boss needs done. Shouldn't get in the way of us acquiring or eliminating the other security companies in town. Or at least stealing their contracts."

"I've been thinking about that. We've been playing too nice. I think it's time to take the gloves off. Instead of being indirect and putting pressure on the casinos to get them to switch to us, we should consider taking out some of the other companies directly."

"Buying off their people?"

"Whatever it takes. Pay them off, put them in the hospital, blow up their houses. We tried it the subtle way, the way the boss seemed to prefer. In the end, I'd guess results are the most important thing. We can get them in a lot of useful ways."

Jared drummed his fingers on the desk. "That's a can of worms, though. If we open it, there will probably be retribution against us in kind."

The dwarf slapped a hand down on the surface between them. "Let them come. Hell, I *want* them to try it. We'll beef up our security and make sure our people are always on guard. We have the advantage here since we know what's going on. That'll give us all the edge we'll need."

He shrugged. "Okay, that works for me. Where do you want to start?"

"Crystal Security."

Jared nodded in complete agreement. "You're right. We should keep the pressure on the Atlanteans, and taking out their contractor is a great way to do it. Who knows, after they almost lost their kid, they might be more inclined than the rest to change."

"Especially if their security company can't protect itself."

Jared grinned. "All right. Let's do it. Tell me what you need."

CHAPTER FIVE

Ruby had dressed formally for the occasion, wearing a blue dress with a broad vertical silver stripe and high boots that disappeared under the long skirt. The thin straps showed off her strong arms and shoulders. Although she didn't wear dresses often, this was one of the few she owned that she thought she looked good in.

Walking through the streets of Kemana MountHaven always felt a little odd since she'd spent so much of her time aboveground, attending human schools, hanging out with human friends, learning the ropes at the casino, and the like. She'd discussed that impression with her siblings, and they had more of a connection to the underground city than she did. That wasn't to say she disliked it, only that she was less at home there than she might otherwise have been.

Storefronts lined the street leading to their meeting place on both sides, none of them more than a couple of stories high. They passed shops that sold decorative works for the home, another that sold weapons, a third that sold potions. Food stores, restaurants, and all of what you'd expect to find in a typical human city, more or less, were also present here. This late at night, the streets were mostly empty. Their destination was the tallest building in the giant cavern, the small palace that was the residence of Lord Maldren, the titular leader of the city. He was, of course, a Mist Elf. Given that her people had founded the kemana, that only made sense.

A pair of wizards stood guard at the side entrance, the one used for business rather than formality, and her father exchanged pleasant words with them before they headed in. She'd been in the building's main audience chamber before and had visited a couple of the rooms that held museum-quality items on display for the public. However, her travels had never taken her into what her father called the business area before now. Stone corridors led eventually to a large room with an oval table occupying at least half of the available space. Five seats were arranged along each long curve, with a singular one positioned at the far end. Each place included a notepad, a pen, and a wine glass. Figures in black uniforms stood on one side holding bottles, clearly waiting until everyone assembled to pour.

Her father pointed her toward a trio of chairs in a corner. "Guest area. Wait quietly until we call you."

She nodded, headed over, and sat to watch as the rest of the Council members wandered in. The group numbered lucky eleven, including their leader, and they represented the races who owned casinos in the city. She didn't know all the names, although she was sure she'd been told them, but recognized Rosalind Caruthers from their meeting a few days before. The witch offered a small smile as she spotted her in the corner, then turned to talk to her colleagues. Ruby also noticed Challen the gnome healer, who nodded at her before he too was distracted.

Ruby flinched slightly when the dwarf she'd last seen running from the warehouse where he'd held the Atlantean captive strode in. She fought to keep her expression neutral as Grentham crossed the room to talk to the hulking Kilomea who stood alone in the far corner. She hadn't realized Margrave's competitor was part of the Council and thought she probably should've paid more attention to her father's discussions of the topic. *Which I will from here on out since I might eventually be a member of this group. Hopefully not anytime soon, though.*

Lord Maldren wore a formal robe that covered him from neck to ankles in purple and gold. He managed to pull it off without looking overly pompous, which was impressive given the outfit's splendor. He called for the others to take their seats and lowered himself into his. When they had all complied, he said, "Thank you for coming, as always." He waved at the uniformed workers, and they filled the wine glasses at each place while the Council members waited in silence. After the servers excused themselves from the room, the leader said, "I see we have a guest today. Is that your daughter, Rayar?" It was an unnecessary question; she was the only human who would have possibly been allowed into the meeting without a great deal of planning and negotiation. Nonetheless, it was polite.

Her father replied, "It is. Allow me to introduce Ruby, my adopted daughter." People at the table nodded at her, and she returned the gesture.

The female Drow spoke in a smooth tone. Everything about her was smooth, from her dark skin to her perfectly straight ashen hair. "Why is she here?"

Her father looked at Maldren for permission, and the man flicked his fingers in assent. "Thank you for your question, Elnyier. Ruby has some information to share about the attack on Andrielle's family."

All the gazes shifted to the Atlantean representative on the Council, Andrielle Chentashe, who she'd last seen on the stage during the event in question.

Maldren said, "Ruby, please say what you've come to say."

She bowed her head respectfully as she rose, then raised her eyes to meet those of the people around the table. "I've heard rumors on the surface from the human authorities. They believe one of the local security companies may have been involved in the attack."

The Drow asked, "Which one?"

She made sure to keep her gaze away from the dwarf as she replied, "Unknown. The rumors didn't say." She and her father had concluded it would be too dangerous to name names in this group. They'd agreed it was enough to bring the matter forward.

Grentham growled, "What authorities?"

Ruby shrugged in his direction. "Not sure. If I had any more specific information, I would willingly share it." He didn't look convinced, but Jailynne Sunshi, matriarch of the family that owned the other Mist Elf casino in town, interrupted.

"What I want to know is what we're going to do collectively to deal with these attacks. It's not likely that the one on the Mist and the other on the Ebon Dragon wrapped it up and now everything is fine." She leaned back in her chair, arms crossed and defiant.

At the head of the table, Lord Maldren shrugged. "As always, these matters are why we gather. Would anyone like to comment?"

Rosalind Caruthers, seated beside her husband Anders, spoke for the casino owned by the witches and wizards. "We believe action is necessary. It's highly unlikely these attacks are random and equally unlikely they'll stop on their own."

Lachsan, the Wood Elves' representative, leaned forward on the table. He had uncommonly short hair for an elf, trimmed within an inch of his scalp. "What do you propose? And what evidence do you have that they will continue?"

Ruby snorted inwardly. Her father had often spoken of how Wood Elves on Earth tended toward inaction in most decision-making. He'd attributed it to the long lives that many of the Oriceran magicals shared, meaning anything that might appear urgent at the moment would undoubtedly pass in a short time relative to their extended existence. Anders, less calm and collected than his wife, barked, "Anyone with eyes can see that something's going on. We've never had multiple attacks on our interests like this, and they seem to be escalating. Robbery, then a poisoning, and a kidnapping." He shook his head in disgust. "If we don't do something visible in response, Magic City will become a laughingstock at best, a ghost town because of fear at worst."

Her father said, "We're looking into increasing the

security presence at Spirits. The challenge is in finding trustworthy personnel."

Grentham smoothly responded, "I know a company with a good reputation." The rest laughed since they were all aware of the dwarf's ownership stake in a security company.

Her father offered a thin smile in response. "Of course you do, Grentham. I don't doubt you'll be contacted by us to submit a proposal, and likely by several others in this room."

Andrielle suggested, "Perhaps we should pool our resources to create a stronger negotiating position for us all. If we all hired the same company, we would be better able to keep an eye on their activities. To share information if anything seems strange."

Bartrak, the representative of the hulking Kilomea, shook his head. His voice was a deep rumble. "It would stretch resources too thin, and we would be in competition for the best. Perhaps we should start our own shared security company instead."

Ruby, who had returned to her chair, was entertained by the interplay of expressions on the Council members' faces. She figured about a third of them were interested, another third dubious, and the remainder thoroughly against the notion. That group naturally included Grentham, who countered, "If you're looking for a reliable company, you need look no further. We have the resources to improve the situation today and the ability to scale up quickly thanks to our contacts in both the magical and non-magical communities." Her father had told her the dwarf was particularly fond of making that point, that his was the only one with owners from both planets.

Lord Maldren waited, but no one filled the silence for almost a half-minute. "All right then. Put that on the back burner. It seems to me that the will of this group is that each casino should undertake to preserve its security." Nods came from around the table, some more reluctant than others. Clearly, despite their shared goal of keeping the city prosperous and safe, the various casino owners didn't extend a great deal of trust to one another. *Why would they? I'd find it hard to trust any of them, based on the little I know. I think that's not a situation that improves with increased knowledge.*

The leader continued, "Our other item of discussion is the proposal from Gabriel Sloane to purchase or lease land on the end of the Strip and build Ely's first human-owned casino." An uproar sounded from the other members, each of them impatient to get their views out and as a result talking over one another. He raised a hand. "I know we've discussed this before, and I'm aware you all are very much against it. Understandably so. However, a new factor has come into play. The human is threatening to invoke the local government, to suggest we are exclusionary."

Grentham laughed darkly. "I don't see a dwarven casino on the Vegas Strip just yet, and not for lack of trying." Heads bobbed around the table, and Challen, who had remained mostly quiet, added, "Nor a gnome casino in Reno."

While they were unable to unify on the question of security, they were very much of one mind against the idea of a human gaming company gaining a foothold in Magic

City. The meeting broke up, and Ruby headed for her father's side, only to be intercepted by the glowering dwarf. He said, "Listen, missy. If you hear any more about who was behind the kidnapping, let me know. It's to my company's benefit to get rid of anyone who's making us all look bad. And that's good for everyone."

She nodded, thankful she'd been in disguise when she'd gone to rescue the Atlantean scion, and suddenly also grateful for the perception that she couldn't have been involved since as a human she couldn't do magic. Her hand lifted involuntarily toward the pendant that helped her maintain her illusion of humanity, and she turned it into an offer of a handshake. "Sure will. Count on me. My father has only positive things to say about your company." That was laying it on a little thick, but he seemed mollified when he shook her hand.

"Very good." He turned and stalked away, and she watched his retreating form, thinking hard. *What's your game, pal? I can't quite see it yet, but I guarantee you, it's not going to work out.*

CHAPTER SIX

With neither an invitation nor a desire to join Ruby at the Council meeting—as if her carrying a cat wouldn't be notably strange in any case—Idryll had requested a portal to the surface before her partner had left. Now she crouched atop a two-story building, scanning the area with her senses. So far she'd become somewhat familiar with the Strip but not nearly as knowledgeable about the buildings that bordered it on the south side. To the north were mountains, and while residences and such held position on that side of the Strip, in her view it was much less likely she would wind up finding trouble there than on this side of Ely's tourist destination.

She was in her tiger-woman form, that being the easiest one to navigate with. Since no one had ever seen her and Ruby together, it posed no risk of discovery. Her partner walked a fine line, choosing to become her city's defender while still maintaining relationships with people she cared for. One slip would put those loved ones in danger. Masks would help, as would Ruby's continuing disguise as human.

She laid on the rooftop and used her magic to create a shell that matched the surface's temperature. Moments later, the security drone she'd heard coming whipped overhead, hopefully failing to notice her. The city relied heavily on technology with cameras and surveillance drones aplenty. She hadn't known what the drones were until Ruby had pointed them out, and had since spent time watching television when she was alone in the bedroom of the aboveground house to learn about the things she might not recognize in her new surroundings.

Idryll had seen stories about the police in their mechanical outfits, with their super-powered weapons for countering magical opponents. She also knew Ely had none of those specialists. Magic City wasn't big enough to justify such a team. It was barely big enough to have a police force, even with big money in the casinos. She wondered if the Council had played a role in minimizing human authority in the city. If she were part of that group, she would feel motivated to do so.

She leapt from her building to the next, landing cleanly in a roll as she moved farther along the street, progressing far slower than she was capable of to get a sense of her new environment. All her forms shared heightened senses, and all of them had magical strength, speed, and stamina. While she doubtless appeared less threatening in this form than as a tiger, the truth was she could do equal amounts of damage with each. She flexed her hands, and the tiger's claws extended from her palms, positioned directly under her fingers and lengthening inches beyond them. She used them to safely climb down the side of the structure, descending to street level. Her eyes could see almost perfectly in the darkness between pools of streetlight glow, and her ears were open for any hint of trouble. She was still sorting out the city's smells, determining what was normal and what was not. That was a work in progress and probably would be for some time as she attuned herself to this particular jungle. That was one of the reasons she'd decided on this midnight stroll.

She felt drawn toward something farther down the block, her instinct for danger twitching a warning. The street she walked was deserted, or else she would've stayed on the rooftops. The sight of her would doubtless spark fear in many of the humans she might encounter on her travels, and she had no desire to do that.

She stuck her head around the corner of a building to peer down another lane. A dim glow spilled out from a doorway, and hushed voices were barely audible. The words they used though, talking of figuring out what was most valuable and exhorting each other to hurry, suggested they were up to no good. She walked slowly toward it, keeping her senses open. The building had a sign on the front that said, "Pawn." She'd seen a television show about those stores that bought and sold a variety of strange goods.

Her nose detected the scent of blood, and her eyes narrowed. Theft was one thing. Her concerns about property were minimal at best unless it was things valued by people she cared about. Hurting others was a different story. She stayed in the shadows across the street but maneuvered until she could peer through the entrance. The broken front door hung from a hinge, which was what permitted the light to escape. A body lay crumpled on the floor a couple of feet inside, likely the source of the smell. Four figures moved within; the number confirmed both by the dim lights they carried and the individual voices. Three were visible, but a shelving unit hid the fourth.

She considered how to handle it. Killing them was out of the question since they hadn't killed the person bleeding on the floor, judging by the sound of the figure's sturdy heartbeat and occasional moans. Nor could she imprison them anywhere, even if she had a reason to do so. *So I'll have to involve the human authorities.* Idryll looked up and down the road, and two doors away saw a store with a window behind a metal gate. She darted across the street, extended her claws and sliced through the barrier, then stabbed them into the glass to break it. She was sure that, like the security company, this business would have an alarm to summon the police. However, she wasn't about to let them have the fun of taking down the criminals in the other building.

Idryll was through the door before the robbers knew she was there. The first shouted in surprise as she neared him but had no chance to defend himself against her attack. She kept her claws sheathed and delivered fast punches to his stomach, chest, and face. The light dropped from his hand and clattered on the floor as he stumbled backward, and she spun into a reverse hook kick, her heel colliding with his head an inch above his ear and sending him tumbling to the floor.

She'd kept her attacks mundane, not using her magic speed or power for fear of hurting her opponents more than she intended. It was a difficult thing to judge, figuring out how much of her potential strength to use. She sensed

Ruby would not be happy leaving a trail of bodies behind them. While Idryll was more or less indifferent to the continued existence of those who would hurt innocents, there was something to be said for giving those who erred a chance to mend their ways and pay their debts to the ones they'd injured. Metal glinted in the beam of light as the nearest enemy pulled a knife from somewhere. It was as long as his forearm, with a serrated edge and a sharp point. Idryll retreated toward the door as she heard one of the others moving in that direction and laughed. "Oh no, you won't get away that easily."

The fourth one, still hidden from view behind the shelf, called, "What's going on?"

The foe who'd been trying to escape had stopped, and he replied, "Some kind of lion creature thing. Damned magicals. Seems to think she can beat all of us."

The man with the knife didn't join in the conversation. Instead, he rushed ahead and stabbed at her with the weapon. She whipped her arm down in a block, striking his hand above the wrist and deflecting the arm off to her left. However, her opponent was cagey and had tossed the knife to his other hand an instant before her strike, releasing his flashlight to catch it. The blade snapped out in a fast slash, and only her quick dodge, throwing her hips off to the side away from it, kept her from serious damage. The weapon scored a shallow furrow in her flesh.

With a snarl, she lifted her leg and pistoned it out with another shift of her core, catching the man in the sternum with a sidekick that hurled him into a nearby wall of shelves. He landed on the floor, and the items for sale crashed down on top of him, along with their supporting wooden surfaces. *Two down.* The fourth man had emerged with a pistol in his hand. He fired, and she dove forward to her right, putting a set of shelves between them and offering the third man a clear path to the door. She leapt into the air over the barrier, using her magic to jump farther and faster than any human could, and although the man tried to track her movement with the gun, he wasn't fast enough and his shots went awry.

She somersaulted in midair and crashed into her enemy with both feet extended, knocking him back against a wall. He was smart and coiled up so his head didn't get smashed and immediately brought up his weapon for a counterattack. She bent over backward into a backflip, then let herself fall to the floor in a roll, avoiding his bullets. He cursed and quit shooting as his partner came in line with the gun as it followed her. The third man tried to punch her as she rose, but she blocked it and spun him around, positioning him directly between her and the fourth, then jumped and delivered a two-footed kick to his chest that propelled him back into his partner. This time the man with the gun didn't protect his head, and it cracked off the back wall. He fell, and the pistol clattered to the floor.

Before the third man could reach it, she stepped up and grabbed him, channeling magical strength into her left side and arm to lift him and slam him back against the wall. She extended her claws slowly to ensure he could see them glistening in the dim light. "Do not think you can act with impunity in *my* town. Hurt my people, and you will get hurt yourself, in double measure." She pulled back her claws before punching him, then ran for the street, scaling the building opposite and perching on the roof as the police arrived in their loud cars with the flashing lights.

She listened to their conversations as they took charge of the situation and heard two things of interest. The first was a confirmation that the shop owner, or whoever it was, was alive and likely to recover. The second came from one of the criminals who'd regained consciousness babbling about how when they got there, the door was wide open and the worker was already down, that it wasn't planned, but rather a crime of opportunity. Idryll frowned, wondering why the door would've been open at night, and thought the situation might be part of something bigger and more interesting. She headed across the rooftops toward the Strip, seeking one of the many hidden ways into the kemana. *Ruby will want to know about this.*

CHAPTER SEVEN

The next morning, after Idryll shared what she'd seen at the pawnshop the night before, Ruby had to see it for herself. She hurried through showering and dressing, then headed for the surface. This time, the tiger woman came along, hidden behind an illusion until she could take to the rooftops. Her partner claimed she could avoid the cameras and the drones up there without a problem, and Ruby wasn't about to start doubting the shapeshifter's skills. *She'll probably smash them if they get in her way, being the subtle creature that she is.*

She strode with a purpose toward the break-in's location. Police tape cordoned off the street on both ends, and uniformed officers rerouted traffic to compensate. Three cars were pulled up outside the pawnshop with their lights off. Ruby spotted the sheriff's hat first, then the rest of her, and walked up to shake Alejo's hand. She'd pulled her dark hair back in its customary braid, but her dark eyes looked tired. "Long time no see, Sheriff."

The other woman chuckled. "You're like a bad penny, Ruby. You keep turning up."

She shrugged. "Just lucky that way, I guess." She took a step closer and lowered her voice. "I hoped you'd be here. I wanted to tell you that rumor on the street says one of the security companies in town may have been involved in the kidnapping attempt against the Chentashe family."

The Sheriff's face went blankly professional. "Source?"

Ruby gestured toward the air. "You know how information flows, drifts, lands for a while, and moves on. This is one of those situations."

"Not much to go on."

Ruby met that flat gaze with a small smile. It was the standard police game, fishing for knowledge without giving any back. "More than you had, I'm guessing." She turned deliberately to face the wreckage of the shop's front door. "Kilomea?"

The taller woman barked a laugh. "No, plain old thermal cord. Burned through around the lock. Not sure why they went after the top hinge, too. Maybe they thought that would be better, then realized the lock would be easier. Criminals." She said it like they were the stupidest branch of humanity.

"What's inside?"

"There was a fight. Some people got hurt. No one died."

Thank goodness for that. "That's a plus, anyway. Anything stolen?"

The sheriff groaned. "Place like this, I'm not even sure how we'd know. It's not exactly pristine inside these types of businesses on the best of days, and keeping a record of inventory is more an afterthought than an actual business practice."

Ruby nodded. She was aware of the financial games played in the pawnshops, where they acknowledged maybe one out of five transactions. It was one of the darker features of living in a gambling town, and the Council kept a very close watch on the most nefarious of those looking to use others' misfortune to their benefit. "Well, that's kind of boring."

The sheriff nodded. "Yep, another normal day in Magic City."

Ruby turned to her with a laugh. "Okay, can we drop the nonsense now? Clearly there's more to it or A) you wouldn't be here, and B) the street wouldn't be blocked off. Unless everything I've ever seen on cop shows has been a lie, there should be more activity here for collecting evidence or processing the scene or whatever." She pointed a playful finger at the other woman. "You're waiting for something."

Alejo shook her head sadly. "Heaven save us from the inaccuracies of cop shows on TV. Ever since CSI came on the air, everyone thinks they're an expert." Their attention was caught by movement at the far end of the street where a black SUV had pulled up. The police officer blocking the way approached the driver's window, then waved the vehicle on. "Then again, you're not wrong. I have to say, I've never seen a case go federal as fast as this one."

Ruby frowned. "Federal? Really? PDA?"

The sheriff shook her head. "Different group. Not sure of their name, just got the word they'd be coming down and we were to hold the crime scene for them." She chuckled. "I hope it's Dralen Caruso. He's the cutest investigator ever."

Ruby figured the rumors she'd shared about the security company had inspired the other woman to share the information she had so far and expected the sheriff to dismiss her. If Alejo had planned to do so, perhaps she forgot in the shock of seeing a woman exit the driver side and open the back door of the SUV, followed by a three-foot troll jumping out of the vehicle, turning a perfect somersault in midair, and landing next to her. The woman shook her head, sending collar-length dark hair swishing, then slammed the door and turned in their direction. A smile graced a strong-boned face, and black tactical pants, matching boots, and a red blouse under a weathered leather jacket that was heading from pure black to a less decisive shade wrapped her body.

The newcomer walked with confidence, clearly an authority figure who expected cooperation. When she and her companion arrived, she stuck out a hand to the sheriff. "You must be Valentina Alejo. You look exactly like your description. I'm Diana Sheen."

Alejo nodded. "You're pretty much what they told me to expect, although no one mentioned you'd be bringing a friend."

Three sets of eyes turned to look at the troll, who laughed happily. "I'm Rath. Pleased to meet you."

Diana smiled down at him. "We've spent too much time on the base lately. When the opportunity for a road trip came along, I couldn't pass it up. Plus, we took a helicopter from Vegas, and he loves helicopters."

Rath clapped his hands gleefully. His spiky purple hair

made her happy to look at, and the wide grin never seemed to leave his face.

The sheriff asked, "What's your interest in the case?"

Diana held up a hand and tapped her ear with the other one. "Yes, we're here. No, we haven't gotten inside yet. Dammit, Glam, chill out." She paused and shook her head. "I don't care if there's a *Fortnite* tournament today. I'm the boss, remember? You work with my schedule, not the other way around." She tapped her ear again and shifted her attention back to them. "My team is demanding but amazing, so you have to let them get away with the attitude sometimes. To answer your question, the woman I just talked to is our head tech, and her computers pinged this event as having a potential connection to one of our investigations. So, here I am."

Ruby decided to be bold and stepped forward while sticking out a hand. "I'm Ruby Achera."

Diana shook it with a nod. "You were in my briefing materials, although I can't remember exactly where. Something about a casino explosion, maybe?"

Ruby nodded. "Yeah, that's me, right time in the wrong place."

Rath said, clearly imitating a tough guy, "You're the wrong guy in the wrong place at the wrong time, McClane."

All three women laughed, as did the troll, and Diana commented, "The more you get to know Rath the more you'll discover that he loves movies. Especially action movies. I swear, at first, he only spoke in quotes."

Ruby replied, "He's not wrong, though. I didn't expect my homecoming to involve a casino blowing up around me. Particularly the one owned by my family's biggest competitors."

Diana cocked her head to the side. "You're related to casino owners?"

"The Acheras own Spirits casino. They, uh, adopted me a ways back. We live in Kemana MountHaven, although I also have a place with some friends up here on the surface."

The agent nodded. "Perfect. I may need to ask you something about the kemana later since we have a task to complete down there, too. For now, let's take a look at the crime scene, with your permission, Sheriff."

Alejo gestured at the pawnshop. "It's all yours, Agent Sheen."

The other woman smiled. "Diana. Trust me; I'm not even slightly interested in taking control of your case. I'm only giving the scene a once-over to see if it can shed any light on my stuff. I have plenty on my plate already, believe me."

She turned toward the building and reached under the back of her jacket, pulling a device that resembled a doubly thick cell phone from underneath. She tapped her earpiece with the other hand. "Okay, Glam, I'm ready to go. Do you have a connection with the scanner?"

Ruby moved up behind the woman, right next to the troll. Until someone told her to leave, she would get as much information as she could. She looked down. "So, you're an agent too?"

He nodded. "Sometimes. Sometimes I patrol on my own or with Max."

"Max?"

He laughed, seemingly joyful about pretty much everything. "Best dog ever. Best partner ever."

Ruby's brain tried to put together the image of the troll and the dog wandering the streets of Magic City looking for wrongdoing, but she couldn't quite bring the picture into focus. She was distracted when the agent started speaking again. "Okay, I'll walk forward slowly. Tell me what you want me to do." A period of silence ensued as Diana moved into the building. She took a single step at a time and waved the device in her hand in each direction before moving on. When she got to the rear of the room, she turned back with a frown. "You're sure? There's nothing to see?" She paused for a minute and replied, "Hang on." She looked around and spotted the sheriff. "Where's the circuit panel for this place, do you know?"

Alejo pointed at an inset rectangle painted the same color as the wall, hidden in a shaded corner. Diana waved the device at it and scowled. "I'm not an electrician, Glam. I don't know." She sighed and put the tool on her belt with a small head shake and muttered something under her breath. Raising her voice, she announced, "Better stand back. This could get a little sparky." She lifted a hand and flicked her fingers at the box, and lightning shot from her fingertips, causing the sparks she'd predicted.

Multiple lights blew out, and a snapping sound came from a portion of the floor. "Aha," the agent said with a grin. "Reveal your secrets." She knelt and felt around, eventually getting her nails under a small panel and pulling it open. She did something inside it, and another *click* came from the corner of the room. Ruby followed her over to the hatch, which revealed a set of steps descending into darkness. Diana stood and brushed her hands off on her trousers. She tapped her ear again. "Okay, we have a staircase. Let's see where it goes." She pulled the sensor back out and pointed down the stairs. "Rath, you're standing guard. No one comes down until I give the all-clear."

The troll replied, "Got it," and turned to face them with a theatrical scowl and crossed arms as his boss started down the stairs.

CHAPTER EIGHT

After a moment, Diana called up, "Clear." The troll bustled down the stairs. Ruby followed on the sheriff's heels, hoping the two women didn't kick her out. When they got into the basement, they discovered a much cleaner and more organized space than above, well lit, with a counter that ran around three walls at stomach height. Displayed there were a variety of magical items including mannequin heads with necklaces dangling from them, small racks with knives, and other arcane bric-à-brac.

Sheen seemed most interested in a trio of spots that stood empty and waved the scanner over them. Presumably replying to the voice in her ear, she said, "Yeah, that's what I thought. Definitely traces of magic here. That spot there might have even contained a Rhazdon artifact, based on the readings. I doubt it, in a place like this, but anything's possible." She paused, listening, then nodded. "I agree there's not much more we can accomplish here. I'll get a good scan of it across all modes before we go, so you can take your time sorting through the data."

Diana set the scanner in the center of the room and gestured for them to stand back. It emitted lights and sounds and generally appeared to be doing things, then felt silent. She retrieved the unit, returned it to her belt, and turned with a grin. "So, since your family lives in the kemana, I'm guessing you can tell me how to get there."

Ruby nodded. "I can do better than that. I'll escort you."

"Much obliged. You folks here in Magic City are far nicer than those in Vegas or Reno."

Alejo chuckled. "You're just getting to know us. Stick around for a while and see if you still feel that way." The comment drew a laugh from the agent and the troll.

They ascended the stairs and exited the crime scene, then said their goodbyes to the sheriff, who looked equal parts bemused and resigned about not knowing what was going on. Ruby felt more or less the same way but hoped that the good deed of helping the agent and her sidekick get into the underground city might loosen up more information. They climbed into the car, and she was amused to see that the troll had a booster in the rear seat. He was simultaneously childlike but not; she was aware that trolls could become enormously strong and large creatures at will, although she'd never seen one do it. Somehow she couldn't picture Rath that way, though. Imagining him doing it beside a dog was downright impossible. *Maybe Max is a mastiff.*

They drove the short distance to Spirits, not because it was the closest access point, but because she wanted to show off her family's business. Something about the other woman made Ruby wish to impress her. *Maybe it's her no-nonsense demeanor or the obvious confidence and competence she projects. Or perhaps it plays into the dream we all have to become a fancy secret agent.* She laughed at herself and filled the drive with small talk.

They handed the car off to the valet and headed up to the management floor. Ruby offered to introduce them around, but Diana declined, explaining, "We're on a pretty tight schedule. I want to be sure to reserve the time we have to meet with our contact below."

So, she took them to the shaft. The sudden surprise realization that she'd have to descend the staircase, which was going to be long and annoying, caused her to fumble her words a little. "You jump down and use force magic to cushion your fall. Indicators on the walls let you know when you're getting close. I'll take the stairs, naturally."

Diana asked, "Is this a secure room?"

The question elicited a confused frown. "Secure enough. No cameras are watching or anything if that's what you mean."

The agent perched on the railing that protected the room's occupants from stumbling into the shaft unexpectedly and said, "I can tell you're using an illusion."

Ruby blinked. "What?"

Diana lifted her left hand and pulled back her sleeve to show a silver bracelet. "This is an illusion detector, a useful tool. I wasn't sure it was you at the crime scene since a lot of people were around, but as soon as we got in the car, it was obvious."

Curiosity overcame the initial shock of being discovered. "That's a very specific device. I haven't heard of those before, and I study magic and technology interfaces."

The other woman shrugged. "I work for a clandestine agency. Not much of what we do hits the papers."

"Maybe I could get a schematic?"

Diana laughed. "I'll hook you up with Glam. I'm sure the two of you will have all sorts of things to talk about. I guess the important question is whether your illusion is a tool or if you have magic instead. Or I guess it could be both."

Ruby decided to trust the agent. *Might as well, since she's already figured most of it out, anyway.* "I'm a Mist Elf. My parents insist on the disguise for safety reasons they choose not to explain." She trusted the other woman enough to share that, but not enough to get into the details.

Diana clapped her hands. "Excellent. Rath, climb on." With a jump up to the railing and another to her shoulders, the troll positioned himself on her back. It was clear the duo had done that before. The agent grinned. "See you at the bottom." Then they jumped.

<hr>

Once they'd sorted out their respective landings, Ruby escorted the pair down the tiers into the bowl of the cavern that held the shops, restaurants, and other commercial enterprises. She asked, "Okay, who are we looking for?"

Diana replied, "Shentia. She's a Drow."

Ruby frowned, reaching back into her memory. "That sounds familiar. If I remember right, she's over to our left, most of the way across the bottom." The name rang a bell as someone who did business in rare magical items. *Makes sense, I guess, given why they're here.* "I think she's only in town sometimes. Like, maybe she has shops in multiple locations?"

Diana nodded. "That would fit."

"Is she part of your case?"

The other woman lifted a hand and waggled it from side to side. "She might have some useful information, but the real reason I need to visit is that a friend of mine asked me to. When this particular friend asks you to do a thing, you just do it because complaining would be both useless and exhausting."

Ruby laughed. "I have one of those. She's my mentor Keshalla, on Oriceran."

Diana broke into a matching grin. "It's about the same here. She's a teacher, a trainer, and probably my biggest critic."

"Sounds *exactly* the same."

Diana shrugged. "Then you know how it is."

A younger voice piped up from behind them, "You know how what is?" They stopped and turned, discovering Morrigan standing there. Rath said, "Woo, sneaky."

Her sister laughed. "Mist Elves are good at veils and illusions. You all were pretty distracted, anyway."

Ruby asked, "How did you know we were here?"

"I saw you head into the shaft room. I was upstairs in security."

"Ah." She looked at her companions. "Agent Diana Sheen, Agent Rath, this is my sister, Morrigan Achera."

Diana smiled. "Pleased to meet you. Be careful sneaking up on us in the future, though. Rath can be pretty dangerous."

The troll made a fierce face and growled, inspiring a round of laughter. Morrigan asked, "Did I hear you say Shentia?" Ruby nodded. "I think you're going to where her shop used to be. She moved recently, a little bigger place ahead and to the right."

Ruby replied, "Hey, you made yourself useful. I bet it's been a while since that's happened."

Her sister stuck her tongue out at her, and Ruby returned the favor as they got moving again. Along the way, Ruby pointed out interesting things she knew about the shops and stores, and Morrigan did the same. Rath asked many questions and wound up deep in conversation with her sister while Ruby sped up to walk beside the agent. Diana said, "Is there a particular reason you were at the crime scene?"

She shrugged. "I had a piece of information I wanted to give to Sheriff Alejo, and I figured she'd be there."

"Seems as if a phone call would've been sufficient."

Ruby laughed, a little embarrassed. "I like to know what goes on in town. It's important. For my family's business, I mean."

Diana shook her head. "I see more than that in your attitude. The business angle is probably a part of it, but not all of it. I won't pry, though. For now."

Thankfully, the conversation ended as they arrived at the door to the Drow's shop. Diana led the way inside, introduced everyone, and exchanged some quiet words with the proprietor. She seemed older, not elderly but definitely in the second half of her years. Nonetheless, her eyes sparkled with interest and intelligence. Once they finished talking, the Drow waved at them all. "You are welcome in my shop. Please, follow me to the back." What looked like decorative objects filled the front room, most of them magical in some way: glowing, moving, or emitting sound or scent. Ruby would've enjoyed getting a closer peek at all of them.

The back room turned out to hold far more interesting items. What they lacked in quantity, they more than made up for with their impressive quality. Each item looked as if it was older than she was and would likely still look that way long after she was dust. Their host walked over to a pair of bracelets, thick silver bands of an unidentifiable metal etched with symbols. She opened the cabinet and pulled out two fabric pieces, wrapping each of the objects carefully before handing them both to Diana. "These are what Nylotte needs. Plus, she hasn't made it out here in person yet, so she probably wanted you to have a direct connection so you can portal in whenever she wants you to."

Diana laughed. "I'm sure that's part of it, at least. The day that Nylotte is working only a single angle will never come."

The Drow nodded. "She's canny, that one."

"And then some." She lifted the bundle. "Thanks for this."

The other woman waved a hand. "Think nothing of it." She escorted them back out and said, "Ruby, I noticed you examining my inventory. Please feel free to return and take a look at any time. Several of them would make nice additions to the Achera residence, I'm sure."

She nodded. "I definitely will."

Diana said a quiet word to Rath once they were outside,

and the troll grabbed her sister by the hand and dragged her off to show her something across the street. The agent shook her head. "He's great, but he's not exactly subtle. Look, it's clear you have more than a passing interest in what's going on in your city. If that gets you into trouble, or if you need anything to make life easier, I can probably help."

The agent dipped a hand into her back pocket and came out with a slightly rumpled business card. "This is my number. You can call me anytime. If I'm not immediately available, it'll connect you with someone in my organization, and they'll know to help you out. Also, a warning. You should pay cash for anything you take from Shentia. If you owe a favor to one of Nylotte's friends, well, you'll probably wind up running errands for them." She lifted the packet and laughed but locked a serious gaze on Ruby's eyes. "Although sometimes the strangest assignments provide the most interesting and unexpected results."

Ruby nodded. "It was great to meet you and Rath. I hope we get to see each other again."

"Maybe I'll come for vacation sometime."

"We can give you the deluxe package at Spirits, on the house."

Diana laughed. "Well, now I'm *definitely* coming. Although someone will need to entertain Rath."

"That's what little sisters are for."

"Perfect."

The agent opened a portal and strode through with her sidekick, who added a jump to his transit. All Ruby was able to see through the opening was a hallway that didn't reveal nearly as much as she would've liked to know about where the duo headed. Her sister stepped up next to her as the rift closed and observed, "Interesting people."

Ruby nodded. "Very."

Morrigan smacked her on the arm. "So, what does she mean when she says you're keeping an eye on what's happening in the city?"

"Nothing. Even if I were, it would be none of your business, nosy pants." *Just what I need, my sister thinking that something suspicious is going on. I'll never hear the end of it.*

CHAPTER NINE

Ruby had made it back to the house she shared with her roommates in plenty of time for dinner and had announced they should all eat as a group for a change. She dragged in a couple of the others to help her cook, and in short order, a good family-style pasta meal was ready to go. They sat in the mismatched chairs around the dining room table and passed the serving dishes from hand to hand. She sensed everyone else was equally pleased with the chance to sit and have a normal meal together. Idryll prowled the floor, getting pats from everyone, bumping into them one after the next. If anyone failed to attend to her quickly enough, they got a leg full of claws. Her roomies found it quite amusing, to judge by their laughter.

Ruby asked, "How are things at the Ebon Dragon after the attack, have you heard?"

Around a mouthful of pasta, Demetrius looked at their resident witch. "You answer. Can't talk. Eating."

Daphne laughed and threw a napkin at him. "Everything seems more or less back to normal. There's more security around, but I'm not sure how useful that is. I suppose they might have more people on the outside of the place too, but if they do, I haven't noticed them."

Liam observed, "Invisible security is probably the best kind of security when you think about it."

Daphne shrugged. "Could be. Anyway, at least those scumbags didn't try to kidnap any of us. Although poisoning, even non-fatal, wouldn't have been a real thrill either."

General assent met that statement. Shiannor said, "They're good people, the owners of the Kraken. I've spoken with them at parties on several occasions. They're not like what you'd think Atlanteans are normally like; they're cool, talkative, and pretty laid-back."

Ruby asked, "That's not how Atlanteans generally are?"

The elf laughed. "Okay, my bad, I was stereotyping. Although it's fair to say the other Atlanteans I've met in my life were a little less personable than the Chentashes."

Demetrius added, "I've worked with Atlanteans on various gigs. I think they're like anyone, some good, some bad, some smart, some dumb. And some really cute." The comment earned playful scowls from the females in the room.

Liam said, "I was hanging out at the Grinding Axes. The crime spree we're having is all the talk there. Someone was taking bets for which casino would get hit next."

Ruby rolled her eyes, but it wasn't a surprise that in a town like Magic City, people would lay odds on just about anything. "Does it seem to you all that things are getting worse?"

Daphne shook her head, and her expression was both supportive and nonjudgmental. "It might be you have kind of a unique view of life here since you're part of a casino owners' family and all, and you've been out of town for a while. Things in Ely have always been rough. There's regular crime, though it's mainly low level. We hear about it all the time. Loners usually, plus some that have banded together to cause trouble."

Ruby frowned. "Gangs? Here?"

Demetrius shook his head. "Teams, maybe, or syndicates, even. Not looking for territory or anything. Not like on *The Wire*." He laughed. "They're out to make money and have discovered it's easier to do when you work with others with the same sense of, or lack of, respect for the law."

Ruby shook her head, half-surprised at the knowledge and half-stunned that she'd never seen it. "What kinds of teams, or groups, or whatever?"

Shiannor replied, "All kinds, really, from what I hear. People at the clubs are always talking about them. You have your petty crime organizations, the ones who do simple breaking and entering, that sort of thing. You got a bunch that exist mainly to prey on the tourists' vices, just like in any party town. There are surely some doing more extravagant things for much higher stakes, although those are more hinted at than obviously visible, at least among the folks I talk to. We've all seen *Ocean's Eleven*. There have to be some people running con games in the city, right?"

Liam chuckled. "I get to be Bartrak Pitt. I like the way he's always eating." He reached out and filled his plate a second time, to the others' laughter.

Ruby replied, "I had no idea. Seriously. I wonder if the Council knows."

Demetrius returned, "I think so. There's enough intervention from the authorities to keep a lid on things, more or less. Obviously, since you haven't noticed, they've done a pretty good job of it. Sometimes it's Alejo, and sometimes it's the local police department, sometimes it's even the Paranormal Defense Agency."

Shiannor interjected, "Speaking of which, there are at least some of those guys in town right now. You can tell them by looking at them. They were out at the club last night. I can't remember which one. I went to a bunch, and they kind of blur together. They walk around like predators, unaware that here, they're prey animals at best."

Daphne laughed. "What are you, part Kilomea?"

The conversation shifted to less weighty matters, and all in all, it turned out to be a pleasant evening despite the eye-opening look at Ely's underbelly. When it was over, Ruby took Daphne aside and asked quietly, "If I were looking for one, where would I find one of those gangs? I think my parents need to know more about this."

The witch gave her a stare that Ruby read as doubtful but replied, "I hear Bloody Blades is a hangout for some of the less rules-bound people in town. If it were me, I'd probably start there."

Ruby had spent another hour with her friends before claiming she needed to sleep, illustrating it with an all-too-real yawn. As soon as she locked the door to her room, she raided her dresser for the darkest outfit she could find—black cargo pants, boots, t-shirt, and leather jacket, then modified her illusion to give her bright red hair and a different bone structure in her face. A quick check of her phone gave her the bar's location, and she dropped the device in a drawer. She was technologically savvy enough to know her movements could be tracked through it and didn't want people knowing her destination. It was unlikely anyone with malevolent intent would be watching, but it was always better to be safe than sorry on such things. She opened a portal to one of the secluded spots she knew near the Strip and led Idryll in her tiger-woman form through it.

Bloody Blades was several blocks away, so she and Idryll took to the high ground. Off the Strip, most buildings stopped at three stories or so, unless they were hotels. They easily avoided the few of those that weren't on the Strip. She laughed inwardly. *I thought I knew a lot about Magic City, but I didn't know about the criminal activity, and I certainly didn't know nearly as much about rooftops as I do now. All sorts of crazy things up here.* She wove through various pieces of mysterious equipment, stepped over spots that looked waterlogged or otherwise dangerous, and winced at the noise of occasional gravel scattering under her feet. *Very different than the top of Spirits' hotel, that's for sure.*

It was almost midnight, so the ambient activity was less than it would have been earlier in the evening, but as in Vegas and Reno, the party in Ely never really ended. Something was always going on. *Apparently, some of them are nefarious things as well.*

They stopped moving when they arrived across a two-lane street from the bar. Ruby pulled the listening device she'd used at the security company out of her pocket and aimed it at the building's exterior. She had no idea who they were looking for, but the interplay of magic and technology in the device would allow her to isolate individual conversations until she found an interesting one. *If we don't get it tonight, I guess we'll be back tomorrow.* It took a solid twenty minutes of listening, of groaning inwardly at players on the prowl and macho men boasting over their conquests, as well as female versions of the same, before she discovered something of interest. The voices were low and rumbly, and two were involved in the conversation. She put her head close to the speaker and motioned for Idryll to do the same.

Voice one said, "It's almost time for the meet."

The other grunted. "Do you think they'll give us any trouble?"

Ruby couldn't make out much from the voices, only that they were both probably male and that they spoke in a way that suggested secrecy, although with all the noise going on around them, she wasn't sure why they bothered. The first spoke again. "Shouldn't be a problem. We've got what they want, they've got what we want, easy-peasy."

The second asked, "Has the boss worked with these folks before?"

The first one laughed. "He doesn't exactly take me into his confidence or anything. I assume they have good references, at least. If they didn't, I'd hope he would send someone more expendable."

The other let out a loud snort. "True that. Let's get a move on."

Idryll was moving for the side of the roof before the thought crossed Ruby's mind. Her partner's prowess impressed her almost to the point of jealousy, as always. Crouching next to her, she stuck her head over the edge and muttered, "I need a periscope or a drone or something."

The tiger-woman observed, "The list of things you need is not exactly short." She phrased the true statement as a playful insult.

"I know one thing I certainly *don't* need, that's for sure. A cat with an attitude."

Her partner laughed, then gave a small *hiss* as the bar's door opened. Two men exited, and she put the voices to faces as the first said, "Car?"

The other replied, "Nah. It's only a few blocks. Let's walk."

She packed away the device and nodded at Idryll. They stayed more or less to the center of the rooftops paralleling the pair, Ruby relying on her partner's innate stealth to keep them on track. *Some kind of locator. That would be handy, too. Plus more weapons.* Trying to face the idea that she might get involved in more scrapes like she had in the past week or so was still difficult to wrap her brain around.

The dwarves ended their walk at a club Ruby had heard about but hadn't yet had the chance to visit. It was called Unicorn, and Shiannor had told her it was one of the prime meeting spaces for magicals at the moment. It lay far enough off the Strip that most tourists would have no idea it existed, and she'd gotten the sense from the elf that humans wouldn't be welcome anyway. They found an alley to drop into, Idryll easily climbing down the wall and Ruby jumping and using force magic to land softly. She muttered, "I'm not really dressed for clubbing."

The tiger-woman laughed. "That's what illusion is for."

"Yeah, but we don't want to be obvious about it, or someone might wonder what we're up to."

Despite that concern, she cast an illusion over them both, putting herself in a slightly nicer-looking version of what she already wore and giving Idryll a long dress, high boots, and no visible fur. Additional touches at the ears and cheekbones gave them both the look of elves, type undetermined. She muttered, "If this goes wrong, if we have the first feeling that things aren't right, we walk out. If we're blocked, we find a corner where I can switch up our disguises." Visually they could resemble anyone, but someone proficient in illusion also had an edge when seeing through others' illusions. They didn't disguise the way you walked or the way you moved in general. Most other things could be influenced, but that was beyond her skills and beyond those of anyone she knew.

She drew a deep breath and cleared her mind of worry. "Okay. Let's do it."

CHAPTER TEN

They approached the door, which was flanked by a Kilomea and a dwarf standing guard, each wearing leather jackets with patches from a local motorcycle gang. Both species had quickly taken to the idea that spending time on the road on motorcycles was an enjoyable diversion, and Ely boasted one of the most diverse magical biker gangs in the country. They were more a "do work for charity" than a "cause trouble" sort of organization, and Ruby had thought more than once that she might like to join them for one event or another. *Maybe that's something I can do now that I'm back.*

Her internal voice suggested, "Perhaps you should concentrate on the moment, chucklehead."

Shut it. She nodded at the bouncers and pulled open the door, gesturing for Idryll to precede her into the club. She felt the pulse of magic from a device in the dwarf's hand, but neither made a move to stop them. In a voice that was barely audible over the muted something that came from the closed door ahead, she asked, "Magic detector, you think?"

The shapeshifter nodded. "Makes sense. They'd probably be more suspicious of anyone who tried to enter *without* magic than those who come in with it."

"I'm sure you're right." The door in front of them opened as they approached, and a wall of noise and light burst from the room beyond. They stepped inside and moved off to the side so Ruby could get her bearings before advancing any further. Her eyes adjusted to reveal a dance club with a huge floor in the center made of panels that glowed in shifting colors. A machine spilled fog over the gyrating figures, and the dancers who were more than a couple of rows away from them were only silhouettes in the mist. A second level ran around the outside of the space, holding tables and providing a rail for people to lean against and watch the bodies moving below. The DJ booth was on the left wall, and the long bar took up the right one. She asked, "Do you see our duo?"

Idryll shook her head. "We'll need to explore."

Ruby nodded. "Well then, let's get our dance on." She led the shapeshifter onto the dance floor, finding the rhythm of the music and moving with it. She made sure to stay close to her partner to discourage others from attempting to cut in with either of them and pushed progressively farther into the club. They moved along the edge closest to the bar since it would be more likely than the other wall to hold their targets.

Idryll's grace and power were on display here, as well. She was an absolute knockout in the illusion Ruby had provided, which was heavily based on her own body and face, and she made a mental note to dial it back a bit in future illusions unless actively trying to draw attention. When they reached the center of the floor, Idryll swept past her in a dance move and said into her ear, "Far wall. A booth."

Ruby spun to keep her partner in view, making it seem like a flirty response, and circled to look in the direction she'd indicated. All she could make out from this distance was the presence of booths along the back wall of the club, on either side of a large neon sign that read "Restrooms." *The good news is we should be able to dance near enough to listen. The bad news is we have another dozen rows of sweaty people to work our way through.*

As they moved, Ruby took mental notes about the magic that the other patrons were using. It was present in such quantity that it made her feel lightheaded. It seemed like everyone on the dance floor had some sort of illusion or magic item working, making their eyes sparkle, their hair glow, or setting off small detonations when they stomped their feet. She'd spent much more time in human clubs than in those catering to magicals in the past, and the ones she *had* visited were far less showy than this one. *I like it.*

They danced their way through the crowd and stopped as soon as their targets' words were audible, which unfortunately left them right at the edge of the dance floor. A dark elf had joined the pair. The Drow wore an expensive-looking suit, opting for elegance instead of flash in a room filled with the latter. She turned her back to him to avoid focusing on him too closely. One of the dwarves said, "We got what you want. Do you have what we want?"

The Drow's voice was smooth and cultured. "I do. You will show me your side first."

She danced a quarter-circle so she could watch the transaction from the corner of her eye. The dwarf on the Drow's left put a fist-sized bag in front of him. The suited figure opened the drawstring and peered inside. With a nod of approval, he slipped the pouch into his jacket.

He said, "Very well." He lifted a briefcase from below the table and set it on the surface, then pushed it over to the dwarf on his opposite side. "I would advise against opening it here. Some things shouldn't be seen, especially by bystanders."

The one who'd taken the case laughed. "We know where to find you if it's not right. More importantly, our boss knows."

The Drow replied, "Indeed. Please leave me to my drink, then." His manner suggested that he wasn't particularly pleased to be dealing with the pair.

The dwarves took the dismissal in stride, standing and heading for the door. Idryll moved without waiting for a suggestion to do so, positioning herself ahead of them as she wove deftly through the crowded dance floor. Ruby followed more slowly, confident the shapeshifter would be able to track them once they got outside and that she would be able to find Idryll.

She hit the street to see a car pulling up in front of the dwarves. With a curse under her breath, she went to a nearby kiosk and tapped the controls to summon one of her own. Fortunately, it arrived within a minute, and the traffic lights kept her quarry from getting too far ahead. The speed limits in this part of town were low, and the self-driving cars obeyed them meticulously. She looked up and out of the window to see Idryll pacing them on the rooftops and had no worries that the tiger-woman would be able to keep up.

After a drive of ten minutes or so, during which they crossed from one side of the southern section of Magic City to the other, the car ahead of her rolled to a stop. She ordered hers to make a turn and head down a couple of blocks, then got out and quickly made her way back. Ruby reached the main street in time to see the dwarves disappearing into an alley beside a pawnshop, crossed the road, and surveyed that passageway for cameras, spotting only one watching the narrow lane. It was old-school, one of the kinds that rotated through a short arc before reversing course, and was mounted on the building itself. She was confident the device would be purely optical and cast a veil over herself to render her invisible to it. Still, she crossed directly under the camera, avoiding its field-of-view just in case. She made her way to the back of the building and turned the corner out of the alley. Idryll dropped to the ground beside her, causing her to jump a little.

Ruby commented, "Interesting that it's a pawnshop again."

Her partner nodded. "It seems as if these places are more than they appear."

About eight feet off the ground was a small window with bars on the front of it. Ruby gestured. "I think we need to look inside."

"Easy enough for me." Claws slipped out from beneath Idryll's fingers, and she scaled the wall in near silence, taking a position on the right side of the window. Ruby again wished she'd brought a device that would let her see remotely, then climbed the old building's cracked brick. It was difficult, and she lost her grip with one hand more than once on the way up, but eventually found a spot she could use to peer through the dirty glass.

Inside were three dwarves, rather than the two she'd been aware of. She recognized the third, and the listening device brought his voice clearly to her. Grentham said, "So, everything went well?"

One of the others gestured at the case on the desk. "Assuming that's what you want, yes."

Their boss asked, "You didn't check it out?"

They shrugged. "You told us not to. So we didn't."

Grentham nodded. "Good people. I'll take a look. Then we can go out for a celebratory drink." The lock *clicked*, revealing an arm cuff that resembled an octopus, the tentacles reaching around to create the space for the limb. He closed the case, seeming satisfied. "Excellent. This is going to make us a lot of money." He stood and gestured them toward the door. "You head out. I'll be with you in a second." When they'd departed, he lifted a panel on the floor and knelt beside it. The angle was wrong for her to see what he was doing, but eventually, a *clicking* sounded and the *clang* of something heavy and metal being shifted followed. He moved out of the way as he secured the safe, which allowed her to confirm what it was, then replaced the floorboard.

He walked from the room, and as she got ready to climb down, one of the other dwarves' voices came over her listening device. "Hey boss, we heard about a break-in at Stanley's place. Was that us?"

"No, although I wish it were. Seems like we have another player in town. Tomorrow, you guys will do the rounds of our other places and make sure our defenses are fully adequate. In the meantime, anything that hurts our competitors only helps us, right?" Laughter and words of agreement faded as they grew further away, followed by the sound of a door closing.

Ruby looked at Idryll and shook her head. "Okay, it seems like we have problems on top of problems here. I need to think about this. Hungry?"

CHAPTER ELEVEN

A restaurant Ruby had always thoroughly enjoyed was a family-owned diner just north of the Strip, not far enough to be in the expensive residencies, but distant enough from the main drag that it wasn't overwhelmed with tourists. She shifted their illusions so they appeared to be humans, albeit different ones than she'd used before, and they selected a seat in one of the many booths that ran around the dining room's exterior.

Waiters and waitresses meandered through the space, giving the right amount of sass and service to keep things light and enjoyable. She ordered coffee, Coke, and a plate of pecan pancakes. Idryll opted for steak and a side of bacon. That earned her a look from the waitress, but then the woman shrugged and headed for the back. Moments later, they had beverages in hand and Ruby wrapped them in an aural shield so their words wouldn't be understandable from more than a half-foot away.

"There's a lot more happening here than I thought. I'm not sure if everything changed while I was at school, or if it's always been like this and I simply didn't see it. Certainly my parents never shared anything about it."

Idryll nodded. "Would they have been likely to? For instance, do you think your brother knows, since you've mentioned he's actively involved with the business?"

She considered the question, then shook her head. "I doubt it. He would've said something about it. He's not all that good at keeping secrets when something's interesting. I'm sure he'd have a plan for how the casino could defend against it, or more likely get an advantage from it." Ruby laughed. "He's definitely a thinker."

Her partner replied, "When things are complicated, it's usually wisest to break them down into their smallest parts. Perhaps you should do that."

Ruby rewarded the comment with a scowl. "I know that. I'm not an idiot."

"Then why do you act like one so often?"

"You know, the stories always say the *venamisha* is a good thing. I'm not sure anyone really understands the potential consequences."

The shapeshifter laughed. "The result is not the same for everyone. You're just lucky."

"Yeah. Luck. *That's* what I'd call it. What are the other results?"

Idryll lifted an eyebrow, which was gold to match her hair. "That would be telling."

Ruby stared hard at her, then shook her head. "I'm not fooled. You don't even know. You're a liar."

The other woman's grin widened. "If it makes you feel good to think so, by all means." She made a small gesture with her hand as if giving permission. They were quiet for a time while Ruby thought. Their meals came, and they remained silent for a time after that while they ate, and Ruby thought some more.

When they finished eating, she said, "All right. So, let's assume for the sake of argument that the first three events are connected. I feel confident about that, although we have no specific proof tying Grentham and his business to the events at the Mist."

Idryll nodded. "Still, it does seem logical. I believe we can make that mental leap."

"So then we have at least two other questions. First, what's up with the attack on the pawnshop, and second, what are Grentham and his dwarf buddies doing under the guise of their pawnshops?"

"That wraps it up pretty well. Also, what's the ultimate goal of the attacks on the casinos? Is it only a move to get more security business? It doesn't seem like that would be worth all this effort."

Ruby sighed. "You're right. That's another big one. I think we can conclude there's some serious danger in the city at the moment. As long as these people are around, there will continue to be danger. Do you think if I shared this information with Sheriff Alejo, she'd be able to handle it?" Part of her wanted that answer to be yes, but not all of her. Maybe not even most.

Her partner shook her head. "Not without a great deal of magical support. Human weapons are no doubt power-ful, at least judging by those I've seen on television, but it would be difficult to defeat magical attackers with them."

Ruby leaned back in her booth and closed her eyes. "I agree. I guess that's why Agent Sheen and her people are around, so they can do that sort of thing at a high level. Still, there's no way they'd be able to spend a lot of time here, assuming they were willing to come in the first place."

Idryll tapped the table idly with her fingers. "The truth is, even if we take care of this particular situation, someone will step up to fill the power vacuum that results. It's a guarantee, just the way of the world." She chuckled. "The way of both worlds, near as I can tell."

Ruby groaned and straightened in her seat again. "You're not wrong, but you need to quit watching so much television." She drummed her fingers on the table as if competing with her partner's taps while considering her options. "I guess I'm also uniquely suited to help. I have a convenient disguise as a human already. I have my family's resources to draw upon, so I don't need to find a job to pay the bills. And I have access to you, and Keshalla, and Margrave."

Idryll added, "Don't forget the Drow you met."

She nodded. "Right. I guess if I was making a complete list of my assets, I have my family who can feed me information, my friends who can do the same, especially Demetrius, and even Abbott Thomas if I need a refuge."

"When you put it that way, it seems like you've already made the decision."

Ruby's reply was interrupted by the arrival of their dessert orders. Idryll had opted for vanilla ice cream that she licked off her spoon in a manner that spoke to her feline nature. Ruby had chosen pie, apple and cinnamon in a perfect homemade crust. It was one of the things she'd always loved best about the place, and she was thoroughly happy to discover its quality hadn't slipped since she'd been there last. She got a coffee refill, then nodded decisively.

"Okay. If we're going to do this, we need to get a lot of things done quickly. We'll need tools, so a visit to Margrave is in order. It would be smart to have magic tools too, so I guess I should see Shentia. Finally, and maybe most importantly, we need to figure out what to do about disguises. We can't count on my concentration holding up illusions in the middle of a fight. The one thing we definitely will *not* do is put my family and friends at risk."

Idryll nodded with a satisfied look on her face. "I knew as soon as I saw you that being around you would be exciting. About time things got started for real."

CHAPTER TWELVE

Grentham's black corporate SUV pulled up at a warehouse fifteen miles outside of Ely, with his phone locked in the signal-proof box and the vehicle's location system deactivated. He opened the passenger door and hopped to the ground, then walked with a brisk stride toward the building's entrance. His driver hustled ahead to open it for him, and he moved through it without stopping. Inside were a dozen mercenaries, hired and delivered by a local infomancer Grentham had worked with on several occasions. The computer-happy witch was satisfied so long as she was well-paid enough to afford the tech she craved, and his lucrative side business in selling magic items ensured he had whatever money he needed to please her. For him, the game had ceased to be about wealth some time before, and he now primarily regarded it as a tool to get what he really wanted: power, and to a lesser extent, status.

As his rented crew gathered in a semicircle around him, his thoughts turned to his absent partner. He wasn't sure if Jared knew about his black-market magic stores masquerading as pawnshops and didn't care in any case. It didn't impact the amount of time or effort he put in on behalf of the business, so the other man had no say in it. He didn't doubt that they would eventually wind up in a showdown over control of the company. He hoped to simply buy Jared out since his partner enjoyed wealth and the women who were attracted to it. *Not the kind of woman I'd want in my bed. I would much rather have someone who wanted me for me than for the pretty baubles I gifted them. Still, anything that keeps him busy and off my back is a win.*

He nodded at the gathering. "So. Thanks for coming, and as agreed, half-payment is being deposited into your accounts right now." Unlike the group that had tried to cause trouble at the Ebon Dragon, which he'd outfitted himself, he'd paid these extra to bring along their toys. The previous outcome hadn't been all he'd hoped for, and the superstitious side of him wanted to change things up a little, like requesting new dice when the ones you were using went cold.

"We have three goals today. Goal number one is to steal everything that looks remotely useful or valuable." While he wasn't obsessed with money, he was also a firm believer in the philosophy of waste not, want not. "Goal number two is to take out anyone who opposes us. If it's possible to do it non-lethally, great. If we can't, not an issue." *People who decide to work for security companies know they're stepping into a risky situation. While they might not have understood the potential for this particular sort of action, that's not my problem.* "Third, we break into their computer system and strip every bit of data we can. Plus, we grab hard drives, laptops, whatever." The mercenaries nodded. He didn't feel a need to share the fourth objective with them since he'd handle that himself.

He looked them over with a critical eye to ensure they were ready. Each wore body armor of a similar type, although the pieces were hardly perfectly matched. He figured some had gotten it from military surplus, and others had probably stolen it. Most of the mercs carried at least one pistol along with a rifle, and many of them sported additional handguns, grenades, and doubtless several other kinds of wicked implements of destruction. "Any questions?"

A man with a day's stubble, dark eyes, and a crewcut nodded. "Do we get a share of what we take?"

Assuming you survive, sure. Grentham had no problem paying what he promised. He also had no problem *not* paying, should someone fall along the way. Professional soldiers such as these would know the drill. He mostly played straight with them because he didn't want to sour his good reputation. *No doubt I'll need more of these people down the road, especially if Jared doesn't feel like being bought out.* "Twenty-five percent, split among you, to be paid after everything is sold." Less professional men and women would have wanted assurances. This bunch nodded in agreement, knowing how the system worked. "Any other questions?"

A woman to his right asked, "Any principals to capture rather than kill?"

He shook his head. "No. Everyone's a target. Except me, naturally, and my guards. I know this goes without saying, but I'll say it anyway. You'll get no games from me, but *play no games with me.* If we do our jobs, we all make it out substantially wealthier. Let's not do anything to mess that up." More nods of agreement gave him an optimistic perspective on the night's coming events.

He clapped his hands together. "Time to move." He waved for them to follow him outside, lifted the burner phone to his ear, and spoke a single word. A moment later, two beat-up vans pulled into the lot, with plenty of room inside for the team. He stepped back into his SUV, which had been stolen from a dealership barely an hour before. "Let's do this."

Their target for the evening was the Crystal Security Company, which had the contracts to guard several of the casinos in town, including the Kraken. They weren't the biggest, but they were in the top three. Grentham had offered the argument that it might make more sense to spread out the targets, but Jared had an obvious grudge against the Atlanteans, for reasons unknown, and wouldn't hear of it. Ultimately, it didn't matter much.

Their boss had deep plans, and he was clearly willing to play a long game, so eventually all the casino owners would get a taste. Grentham frowned as he wondered what the person who'd come into town on the private jet at the boss' request was up to. He didn't like to think their employer would detail someone to watch them, but so far the people he had out quietly watching for the newcomer hadn't reported any direct sighting or other evidence of him. *Maybe the chucklehead is taking a vacation before getting to work.* Grentham shook his head. *Too damn many unknowns going on in Magic City right now. I'm against it.*

Their target was in a different office park than their company occupied, but it could have been built from the same template. A high chain fence surrounded it, with a decorative grassy area filling the space between the outer barrier and the building itself. Doubtless there would be defenses seeded in that expanse, more likely technological than magical, but one could never be sure. Either way, his team was prepared to handle whatever the other bunch might have come up with.

The structure was three stories high, metal-skinned, and free of windows except on the top floor. The blueprints his infomancer had acquired indicated the ground level held only a garage, equipment storage, and a wide open space that was probably a firing range or other training ground, plus the lobby area. Above it lay conference rooms, offices, and other public-facing spaces. The top level was home to their executive suites, for sure, and also their computer center, if the power distribution system hadn't changed. He and Jared had discussed a surgical strike to that level, focused on stealing data and information, but that wouldn't necessarily take the other company out of the game. So his current plan was to breach at the bottom and let half of his hired guns clear it. At the same time, he and the rest would go up to the second story and take out any defenders, then he and his two bodyguards would take care of the last floor, which they presumed would be lightly guarded.

Although they'd tried to keep news of the incursion into their headquarters quiet, nothing was ever truly secret for long in their small corporate community, and word had inevitably gotten out. Thus, he expected to find this place better defended than it might have been a couple of weeks before. That also didn't worry him. He would follow the people he'd brought, and should the need come for him to play a role in dispatching the defenders, he would be more than happy to get his hands dirty. The mercenaries had selected one of theirs to act as lead, and Grentham walked beside him ahead of the rest as they approached the fence. They had all added masks or balaclavas to their wardrobe to ensure anonymity.

Everyone wore headsets tied to a secure comm system to coordinate their activities when they split off to their various assignments. They approached from the west side of the building, which offered them the most cover. They'd overflown the place a day earlier with a drone and had sent several cars past the location as well to ensure good reconnaissance. Their first concern was the cameras mounted on tall poles inside the fence. They stopped walking at the maximum distance they could manage, and one of the mercenaries lifted a suppressed rifle. She sighted carefully, pulled the trigger three times, and destroyed the ones that might have had an angle to capture their image.

That would provide their enemies the first indication action was underway, and now events would happen quickly. They shifted into a jog, which meant Grentham almost had to run to keep up and arrived at the fence without a problem. A device arced through the air over his head, tossed from behind by one of the mercenaries, and struck the barrier's metal surface. The electrified fence shorted out with a *bang* like a firework exploding. Two mercenaries were there instantly with bolt cutters, snipping a rectangular door for them to pass through. Lights mounted on the building illuminated as they moved through in single file. Grentham snapped, "Alarm status?"

The infomancer's voice came back across the line. "No problems. I have all communication from the facility locked down. No messages in or out."

"Good work. Keep it up." Gunfire erupted from the building, and everyone dropped to the ground except Grentham, who waved a hand to summon a force shield in front of him. They'd expected this too, and he focused his mind to widen the protection and make it tall enough to handle volleys from the top floor if they came. The mercenaries arranged themselves into a line at his back, and one stepped up next to him with a wand attached to a small computer held in his hands. The dwarf walked at a steady pace toward the building, moving laterally to avoid traps the man beside him searched out. Grenades from those following set off those they couldn't escape.

The force shield intercepted bullets that would otherwise have shredded them as they moved deliberately toward their target. He'd feared machine guns but had predicted that level of overkill would be unlikely. The defenders had automatic rifles at best, based on the sound the weapons made and the timing of the pauses for reloading. They appeared to be firing out of gun ports though, which meant his people had no way to counterattack until they got close enough that the angle would be prohibitive for those inside. By the time they arrived there, Grentham was starting to ache from the burden of holding up the shield. Each bullet strike drained a little of his energy, and after a while, each impact felt like a bee sting on his body. Now that they'd reached the side of the building, it was time to choose their attack vector.

The mercenary in charge made the decision. "We're already loud, so we might as well go in the front. Defenses will probably be weaker there than in the garage." Grentham wasn't sure he agreed but also wasn't interested in arguing the point. He followed the man and patted the pocket of his black leather jacket, confirming the presence of a healing potion and a smaller energy potion. The first would be enough to heal almost any damage he'd take, and the second would give him an essential boost if he ran low. His bodyguards, always nearby, knew to administer them if he was incapacitated.

They marched up to the building's front entrance. It had an effective security airlock, with easily bypassed glass doors on the outside, but a small vestibule with a heavy metal gate blocking passage beyond it. Fortunately, they'd come prepared for that. Grentham created another force shield to protect them from the defenders in the lobby while two of the mercenaries wrapped sections of the bars with thermal cord. They looked away, the incendiary burned through the metal, and the real fight began.

CHAPTER THIRTEEN

As the mercenaries pushed back the smaller number of defenders in the lobby with a barrage of gunfire, Grentham barked, "Krista, are you in?" The plan had been for their infomancer to move on to hacking the security system after taking out their communication systems.

The woman's voice sounded annoyed, likely with herself rather than with him. "No. They have magic protection on it. You should probably watch out for other magical defenses."

He muttered a curse and pointed at a door marked "stairs" that led to a fire escape route. Two of his six mercenaries ran ahead and planted a small charge on the lock, which detonated a moment later and caused the barrier to swing free. He followed them up a couple of steps, then danced backward as they clattered down toward him, falling under a hail of bullets. He waited for them to crawl off the stairs, saw no bleeding to worry about, and summoned his force shield again to lead the way. When the defenders discovered their rounds weren't getting through his protection, they tried a grenade. He flicked his fingers and sent it flying back before it covered half the distance between them. It exploded with light and sound that didn't affect his people at all. He charged forward as his foes stumbled in retreat.

Grentham led his team out onto the second floor, but rifle fire from all directions forced him to crouch and scurry to the side. He ducked under his shield in the corner, easily protecting himself from the onslaught, and watched as the mercenaries advanced. They sought cover immediately, and most of them found some, only one of them dropping bonelessly after a bullet struck him in the head. Return fire came from all around until the mercenary leader growled, "Right flank, go." The trio on that side flicked their rifles to full auto and charged behind a fusillade of bullets.

The defenders sailed grenades out at all of them. He sent several of the explosives flying away but couldn't protect the threesome that had advanced from his right. This time the enemy had selected fragmentation canisters, and shrapnel flew as they detonated to drop that trio to the sound of screams of pain.

Grentham cursed and stood, taking advantage of the distraction to advance. Their foes were firing from the mouths of hallways that doubtless led back to offices and the like. He reached out with a line of force to grab a file cabinet resting along the far wall and hurled it into the hallway the fallen mercenaries had been targeting. He dashed forward in the confusion that ensued and followed it up with a lightning attack that sent forks of electricity sizzling through the opening. When he dropped the spell, four defenders were down and immobile, their body armor smoking.

Shooting sounded from the other hallway, reassuring him that his crew was doing their job. He wrapped himself in a personal force shield positioned about an inch away from his skin and walked through the offices, opening each door and checking to be sure no defenders hid inside. Reports came over the radio as the mercenaries cleared the bottom floor, taking casualties but making progress. When he was comfortable the second level was secure, he went out and collected his guards, who he'd tasked with defending the stairwell, and the trio headed up to the third floor together.

The radio signaled that the mercenaries had shifted into collection mode. They'd be stealing anything that wasn't nailed down and more importantly to him, breaking open computers to get at hard drives. However, what he craved was most likely to be upstairs. He wanted the business secrets, the things that would allow him to compromise all their operations if they tried to continue. To make them realize it would be better to call it a day, knowing how vulnerable they were. *If they want to try to make a go of it afterward, I'm more than happy to slap them down.* He stopped first at the server room. His guards blew a hole in the door to permit access, and he connected a small black box to the equipment rack with several ethernet cables. He asked, "You in?"

The infomancer responded a moment later. "Yeah. I have it now."

"What do you see?"

He hadn't destroyed the internal security cameras

because he'd figured they might be of use, although he'd hoped that they'd have this intelligence earlier on. She replied, "Looks like all the defenders are down. I'm unlocking things now." Faint *clicks* sounded from down the hall as the doors unlatched.

He nodded. "Very good. Copy everything you can." He pointed at his guards. "You two, wire this place to blow." He turned and headed toward the offices. A pair of them shared this floor, one for each of the company's principals. He was a little miffed at the fact they were both larger than his space and put that on the list of things to consider later. He entered the right-hand office and stood in the doorway with his fists on his hips. "If I was a hidden safe, where would I be?"

A shiver ran down his spine, giving him enough warning to dive to the side as a ball of fire slammed into the place he'd occupied and set the drywall aflame. He rolled up to his feet, wondering in the back of his brain if his force shield would've been adequate to defend against the attack while he sought its source. A wizard stood in the far corner of the room, where he'd doubtless been hiding behind a veil. The wand pointed at him, and another ball of fire shot out, but this time he was prepared for it. He summoned a second force shield and angled it before him, deflecting the ball up and away rather than trying to block it. It hit the drop ceiling and lit that on fire as well. Grentham charged the other magical, figuring that like most wizards he knew, his foe's preference would be to fight from a distance instead of close up. Personally, either option worked for him.

The mage tried lightning next, and the attack's power

crackled through his shield. His teeth clenched against the stinging pain—he hated lightning with a passion, at least on the receiving end—and kept moving forward. He wasn't sure what his enemy expected, but from the way his eyes widened the moment before the dwarf crashed into him, it wasn't someone ramming into him. Grentham had the angle and the strength, and he blasted upward at the last second, his strong leg muscles propelling his shoulder up into the wizard's sternum.

The man slammed back into the wall with a loud *crack*, then stumbled forward. Somehow he managed to hold on to his wand and swiped it across in a frantic defense. The beam of shadow it emitted slammed into Grentham and burned through his shield in an instant. His shout was as much in anger as in pain as it savaged his right leg. He went down on one knee and growled, "Enough of this shit." Reaching out with a line of force, he grabbed the heavy mahogany desk that was the room's dominant item. He made a whipping motion, and it flew across the intervening space to slam into the wizard. The man rebounded off the tall windows that filled one wall, confirming they were thick bulletproof glass. *See, it's good that we didn't try to come in that way.* This time the mage dropped his wand and crumpled, ending the fight.

Grentham tapped his comm. "Okay, people. Five minutes and we're out." The magical would probably have had the means to communicate with the building's owners, and if so, reinforcements would be on the way. Plus, there was the not-so-small matter of the fire spreading along the wall and ceiling.

Grentham downed the healing potion and grimaced as

the missing flesh in his leg re-grew. "Damn, that itches," he muttered and staggered to his feet. He used force magic to punch holes in the walls at one-foot intervals until he revealed the location of the safe he knew had to be there. Fortunately, the fire hadn't yet reached it. Even better, the lock was electronic. He attached another device, and his infomancer overrode the code and popped open the door.

Physical files sat inside, kept company by a stash of currency and a transparent bag full of gems. He grabbed everything he could and headed for the exit. He linked up with the mercenaries along the way, and once they got back outside, Grentham ordered his guard to blow the computer room. It detonated with a loud explosion, and he spent the next three minutes creating and launching fireballs into the building to ensure all of it was aflame. Once convinced that no amount of fire trucks could save it, he followed the others in a jog to their vehicles. *Objective four complete. All in all, not a bad night's work.*

CHAPTER FOURTEEN

Goryo had timed his action to coincide with the efforts of the people from the security company. He'd left behind a pair of transmitting devices, one in the SUV that picked him up at the airport and the other in the garage that housed the vehicle he'd borrowed. They'd provided enough information to reveal that they were making a move tonight, so he planned his for the same time, figuring that two simultaneous attacks would sow additional discord and confusion.

His role in Ely was a simple one: raise the mental stakes for the casino owners, and cause them to worry. That worry would push them into hiring more security, a service that would doubtless be compromised by his employer's people. He didn't care about that part but had nonetheless figured out the ramifications of the bigger picture shortly after receiving the message seeking to hire him. Goryo worked for the highest bidder. He had no particular concern over plans or goals unless he could either profit from them by investments based on insider knowledge, such as when he eliminated the CEO of a major corporation and sent their stock tumbling, or when it might endanger him at an unacceptably high level. He stayed away from operations involving the organizations he'd associated with in his early career, as several criminal enterprises would take it poorly if he acted against them. Since he frequently used them for supply and other assistance, to oppose those groups would be a foolish choice indeed.

The assignment hadn't specified how he was to accomplish his task, an arrangement Goryo preferred. Without a specific goal other than wreaking havoc and causing trouble, he had the opportunity to select his target. The prior operation suggested that his employer prioritized moving against those with families. It was logical; endangered adults were more or less commonplace, but endangering those who had not yet reached adulthood was universally more threatening. He had never married or had children, and such things did not touch him. However, he understood in the abstract that others felt strong emotions around those issues, and was more than willing to take advantage of the opportunities that vulnerability offered.

Aside from the Atlanteans, who he rejected for the moment based on the prior failed action and his awareness of the security company's plans for the evening, only two other families had children in vulnerable positions. Most of them kept their progeny in the underground city where he couldn't get at them, or at the very least would be incredibly obvious during the attempt. However, the adopted girl from the Mist Elf casino was frequently seen aboveground, as was the entire family that ran the Deep

Woods casino. More elves, this time the forest kind—Wood Elves, they called them. He didn't have much knowledge about that particular branch of magicals. It was enough to know where to find them, and his research had revealed an unfortunate—for them—predictability to their movements.

His raid on the pawnshop provided the primary tool he planned to use for the attack. In addition to his standard gear, which consisted of a sword on his back and pistols strapped to his thighs, the magical weapon he'd retrieved was a pair of batons that screwed together into a large staff. Each end discharged magic when it struck. One delivered a force blast that could knock a target away, and the other sparked with lightning. While he could've found non-magical options to accomplish both those things, the magical ones offered an advantage. In his experience, magic defenses performed better against technology than they did against opposing magic. Since he'd probably have to fight through a decent amount of security, he needed every edge he could get.

He'd stolen one other item from the pawnshop, a small metal disc currently secured to his belt to be his escape route if his plans went awry. It would spill out a line of force as long as necessary to reach the ground, according to his research. He hoped not to have to rely on it but believed in backup options. *And carrying a rope that would extend fifteen stories down would have been pretty obvious.* He'd purchased the other magic item, the one he planned to use when events in the city came to a head. It was waiting for him at the house he'd rented on the outskirts of town through an untraceable third party.

He kept an ear to the ground for rumors of magical items and paid well for people to tell him what they heard. He'd assembled a relatively extensive list of purely magic objects and others that blended magic and technology. Sometimes, he contrived to have them delivered to the place where he was working, where he would then steal them to avoid any paper trail. Other times, he simply bought the items or took them from whoever had them and brought them along to the job himself. A couple more from his list were currently in Ely, one of them an extremely volatile device he'd played no role in bringing to the city, but that he wasn't sure he'd be able to leave without collecting against future need.

His watch vibrated as the moment arrived. The self-driving van he'd rented for the evening rolled ahead at his command and dropped him off at the rear bottom floor of the hotel portion of the Deep Woods casino. He slid out the back, a dark figure in black boots, tactical pants, and a t-shirt with a grey windbreaker thrown over his shoulder to cover the sword's pommel. Hidden beneath it all was custom form-fitting body armor. He strode quickly to an unremarkable door to the hotel. His recon had shown that the Deep Woods used electronic locks on external doors, and he could always buy a tool to break through those if money wasn't an object. The fee for his involvement in Magic City had ensured it wouldn't be.

He placed a rectangular block box on top of the keypad and was rewarded a moment later with a *click* as the latch disengaged. He swept through into a service stairwell. Ahead of him, a long hallway led to kitchens, storage, and probably eventually to the casino itself, with other hallways branching off in both directions. This staircase was for the serving crew to access the banquet rooms on the second, third, and fourth levels of the hotel with ease and without being seen. He walked unhurriedly up the stairs, his senses alert for any potential security alarm, especially for security cameras. He nodded as he passed a pair of tuxedoed elves, who looked young even for their kind. His research indicated the hotel was hosting multiple banquets that evening, including a wedding party of several hundred people. The activity had been one more thing that made this particular night a good one for his maneuver since it would be easier to hide among a larger crowd. The real challenge would come once he reached the fifteenth floor.

After the fourth level, the style of the stairway changed, becoming narrower and more utilitarian. The building's blueprints had shown it as a fire escape, and that's what it seemed to be. He'd chosen this route because it limited the likelihood of running into anyone and would likely be lightly monitored by security. Still, it *was* part of a casino, so dome cameras were positioned at intervals starting at the fifth floor, where the activity from the banquet levels wouldn't be a distraction.

Fortunately, he'd come prepared for that situation, as well. From the small of his back, he retrieved an airgun and a palm-sized monitor. The pistol was bulkier than a standard version and reminiscent of a children's toy that shot rubber bands. Instead, this one almost silently launched tiny electronic chips contained in a putty capsule. He slid the gun through the railing of the next flight up, where the only thing visible would be his arm, and aimed it using the small lens that fed back to the monitor.

He fired, and the device stuck to the plastic shield. It would interfere with the internal electrical processes of the camera, rendering it useless. Moving faster, he picked off the cameras on each of the floors as he reached them. He shoved the gun into his belt at the small of his back after taking out the one at fifteen, then readied himself for the fun part of the evening. A negligent toss got rid of the jacket, which couldn't be traced to him, and he checked to be sure his sword was loose in its scabbard. After verifying the draw on his pistols, he pulled the pieces of the baton out from where he'd hidden them in his thigh pockets, threaded them together, and spun the staff through a figure eight to loosen his wrists. While the guns would've been the more comfortable choice, he wanted anyone who investigated this incident to know that magic was involved. It might suggest that the perpetrator was a magical, shifting attention away from Goryo.

He drew a black mask from his back pocket and pulled it down over his head to ensure no one would recognize him. If a camera had picked him up despite his precautions, it still wouldn't be the end of the world since he wore enough makeup to change the lines of his face and had colored his naturally light hair with a dark dye. Still, he doubted he would have made such a mistake. After all the experience he'd accumulated, such blunders were rare. He grabbed the lock-breaking device, set it over the keypad, and drew a breath as the lock *clicked.*

With a small prayer to fate to be good to him, Goryo flowed through the door, ready to find and kill the casino owners' bodyguards, the casino owners, and their son.

CHAPTER FIFTEEN

Goryo would have chosen to stay in the staircase to the floor where his targets were, but construction permits that he'd dug through showed plans to seal off the stairs at fifteen. If it had been him, he would've let it continue up there but added significant monitoring and traps at that level, in addition to bricking over the entrance. *Better to catch people like me.* So, he had to endure the harder path. Fortunately, violence was one of the few things in life he truly enjoyed, aside from high-quality food and expensive wine. Having to cut through lesser security would be more a gift than a bother.

The hotel formed a large L-shape, a common design on the Strip. He had two routes to reach the sixteenth floor, either the single elevator that included that floor among its stops or a staircase identical to the one he'd ascended that ran along the building's opposite side. Doubtless several of the rooms on this floor would be security posts to keep an eye on anyone making the transit. His preferred option would have been to get into the elevator shaft and climb one floor up, but he was positive any security company worth its contract would have parked the elevator car on that level to block such an approach. If they hadn't, surely the owners' security guards would have. So, it was the long way around.

He walked briskly, not willing to run until they discovered him. He paid particular attention to sounds from behind since smart guards would wait for him to pass before emerging and engaging. Latches *clicked* in front of and behind him when he was halfway down the corridor that ended in a right turn, the signal he'd awaited. He spun and ran back in the direction he'd come, on the assumption that the defenders would expect the opposite. The move surprised the pair who had stepped into the hallway, and they managed only a single missed shot each before he was on them. He rammed the staff forward horizontally, slamming it into their chests and knocking them backward. He pulled it back and rotated it to a diagonal, then whipped it out in a strike at the one on his left. It smashed the man in the temple and lightning blasted out to form a corona around his head, rendering him unconscious at the very least. He fell hard.

Goryo wasted no time assessing the damage but snapped his right leg out in a kick to the other man's groin. The top of his boot met body armor, but the blow was still hard enough to lift the man onto his toes. He flipped the staff in a fast attack, and the tip struck his opponent in the chest. The force blast it discharged hurled his foe ten feet backward, and he hit the floor with an audible *thud*, losing his weapon on contact with the unyielding surface. *One down, one probably down.*

Bullets slammed into his armored back, hitting like punches. He grunted under the blows and forced himself to duck and spin toward the danger. Two more guards were ahead of him, and he was sure that more would put themselves in the path to his objective. He hurled the staff like a javelin at the one on the left, and that woman stopped firing as she danced aside to avoid it. Without breaking stride, he pulled both pistols and fired, several hits knocking the other guard down. He shifted his aim to the woman as she halted and raised her gun, and they traded rounds. His blasted her in a knee, and she dropped with a scream. Hers crashed into the body armor over his heart and ripped a furrow in his left arm below one of the defensive plates. The impact wasn't enough for the bullet to have stayed inside him, so he ignored the light wound. He gave them each a kick to the head to keep them down, reloaded his weapons, and holstered them. He scooped up his staff and charged for the corner. *That's four.*

He rounded it and ducked back immediately as bullets flew. He'd gotten the look he needed, though. The nearest enemies were about ten feet ahead, with another rank behind them at the stairwell door. The guards on the floor above would be faced with a difficult decision, whether to abandon their charges and meet him here, to flee with them, or to stay put. He was gambling on them thinking they were adequate and judging that trying to escape was probably a trap. *Because surely no one would be crazy enough to undertake an attack like this on their own.* His greatest fear was that they'd built an off-the-books panic room. His infomancer had found no records to suggest such a thing, and he figured they would count on their magic being sufficient to protect them. *They're in for a surprise. This isn't my first fight with magicals.*

He went low around the corner, ran in a crouching zig-zag, and broke into a slide as fingers tightened on triggers. Their bullets went over his head, and his move put him close enough to whip the staff across in a low strike. The force tip slammed into the ankle of the one on his left, shattering it and propelling the man bodily into the guard beside him. Goryo was up and running again in an instant, accepting that he had to leave two potential enemies behind to close the distance to the next and trust his body armor would be adequate to any attack they sent. *Four down, two questionable.*

Several more hits struck him from the ones ahead, and he grunted in pain as a rib cracked from a lucky shot. He'd spent years learning to control his body and now put that knowledge to use, pushing the pain into the back ground and dispatching the duo with quick strikes from each tip of the staff. He dropped that weapon and drew his pistols, finishing off the two nearest him and shooting at the pair he'd left farther down the hallway. When the guns clicked empty, he ejected the magazines and replaced them with the special ones he'd been carrying in his back pockets. The likelihood was that he would face magicals on the next floor, and these bullets were espe-cially for them. They were inordinately expensive, so he paid people he knew to identify shipments of them, which he then intercepted. *Cheaper, and more fun.* The fact that this batch would be traced back to an order from the Paranormal Defense Agency gave him no small measure of amusement. He holstered his left gun and picked up the staff in that hand, then went through the door to the staircase.

He threw himself immediately to the side as a bolt of shadow magic sought him. The elf who had shot it stood on the landing above, looking unconcerned with his defense, his right arm positioned in front of him as if it held a shield, his left, the source of the magical attack. *Force shield, probably. Too bad for him.* The angle was perfect to pull the trigger and put a bullet through the protection and into his foe's forehead. The anti-magic round passed through the magical defense like it wasn't there, but his opponent got lucky. Instead of penetrating, the bullet knocked him backward and glanced off to slam into the wall. Either way, the defender was down, and that's all that mattered.

Goryo delivered a kick to his temple as he passed, ensuring he'd stay down, and made it up to the next floor. He paused for a moment to draw a deep breath, then yanked open the door and dove forward in a roll. Electricity sizzled over his head, reaching down to prickle at his spine as he went under it. He wobbled up to his feet to find another elf in a business suit facing him. That one was already sending a second attack, a shadow bolt that Goryo spun sideways to avoid. His foe launched magic with both hands, throwing power like punches.

He kept moving, unable to draw a bead on his opponent as he did, but also narrowing the distance between them with each step. When he got into range, he used the staff to good effect, stabbing the electrical end up toward the elf's head, then reversing the force end into his shins when he blocked the first attack. While his one-handed blow itself was weak, the magic blasted the other man from his feet, and Goryo put a bullet in his torso as he passed. Another guard tried the same strategy and met the same fate. Then he was around the corner into the area that held the family's suites in the hotel.

Only two doors were present in the long hallway. The one on the left led to the public social areas. The one to the right accessed bedrooms, the private kitchen, and so forth. At this time of night, either they would already have been in the bedroom area, or the alarm would've sent them there. He ran ahead and used the device to unlock the electronic door, then pushed his way into the room at a dash. His infomancer had identified the number of people on the family's security staff, and by his mental count only two remained. The first was waiting for him in the large sitting room and was on him the moment he entered. Goryo stumbled to the side, not having expected to be physically attacked, and fell against a tall leather chair. He straightened and used forearms and shins to block kicks and attacks from the pair of knives his opponent held. The bodyguard was good, possibly as good as anyone he'd ever faced hand-to-hand. His foe used magic to increase the speed and power of his moves; an edge Goryo couldn't match.

What he had in abundance was experience. He'd fought off frenzied assaults before, and although he'd had to drop his staff to protect himself, he was never unarmed. The initial flurry gave him a sense of his foe's rhythm, and he broke it with an elbow smash to the elf's cheek. He accepted a cut from the knife in return for the block he'd sacrificed, drawing a line of fire from his right elbow to his wrist, but it took the elf a moment to recover. In that instant, he stabbed a spear hand thrust into his opponent's throat, breaking the vital bones that allowed his foe to breathe. He took one of the knives from him as the other man fell and stomped toward the door the guard had been closer to, figuring that's where the family would be.

The building's fire alarm went off suddenly, and he cursed at whichever one he'd left alive behind him that had activated it. As soon as he started opening the door, a force blast slammed into it from the opposite side, shattering its hinges and slamming him and the door back into the sitting room. He landed on a coffee table, which splintered underneath him, and rolled to the side with a groan. Goryo dipped a hand to his belt and flipped open a small container, grabbing the lozenge that fell from within. He put it in his mouth and bit down, closing his eyes momentarily as adrenaline surged through him, bashing away the pain of his damaged ribs, the slice on his arm, and the beating he'd taken from the heavy door.

He popped up and ran in an arc toward the opening, keeping out of the line of sight of whoever was beyond it. A part of his mind dedicated itself to ticking off the seconds the drug would keep him going. It lasted five minutes, and he would either have to take another dose or be in a safe space for the ensuing crash. Two doses were all he could survive, and he'd far prefer not to have to take the second. He dashed into the adjoining room and dove forward in a roll, drawing the sword as he rose to his feet. Belatedly he realized he'd left the staff behind, but it had done its job in getting him here and suggesting that the attacker might be a magical. He'd pick it up on the way out.

His foe was another of the damned elves, and this one wasn't interested in a fistfight. He conjured a cone of fire at Goryo, and he rolled to his left to avoid it. He cut back in the other direction to dodge the next attack, but the electrical blast caught him full-on and dropped him to his knees in involuntary twitching. The magical kept up the assault as Goryo crawled forward, trying to get close enough. The elf laughed. "Pitiful. Impressive that you got this far, but to have been defeated at this last moment is probably a more painful and appropriate end."

Keep talking, scumbag. Goryo had trained for this. Had paid magicals to hit him with their blasts, discovering which he could handle and which he couldn't, which gear would stand up to it and which wouldn't. Finally, he was close enough. He lunged forward and whipped his left arm, which he'd been dragging as if it was broken, around in a shallow arc to stab the knife he'd stolen from the one in the outer room through his foe's foot and into the floor. The elf screamed, his attack faltered, and Goryo rose smoothly and scraped his sword edge across his opponent's neck.

He left the bleeding foe behind and drew his left pistol, then kicked open the thin door separating him from the next room. It was a bedroom, probably the parents' to judge by the size of the bed. The family huddled in the corner that was farthest from the door and the windows that made up the far wall, dressed in sleep clothes. They moved as he entered: the father charged toward him, the mother raced toward the far side of the room, and the kid dove under the bed. Goryo shifted his aim to the oncoming man and stitched the husband with bullets that easily penetrated whatever shield he'd conjured.

He traversed his pistol toward the woman, catching her in the leg before she got to wherever she was going. She tumbled off the mattress and landed on the floor, out of sight. He circled to finish her off, and suddenly the bed flew at him, smashing him in the hips and propelling him at the window. It shattered as he hit it, and he dropped both sword and pistol as he grabbed for the lip of the floor. He dug at his belt for the disc and slapped it against the side of the building, then pressed on it to eject the force rope. The line glimmered as it descended, and he turned his attention back to the room, ready to lever himself up and deal with the survivors.

The kid had other plans. His face was a mask of pain and hatred as his bare heel came down on the fingers of Goryo's left hand, smashing the small bones and causing his grip to slip. He let go with the other hand before the boy could repeat the attack and reached out for the rope, grabbing it and wrapping his other arm around it to control his speed. His mental clock showed a little under a minute before he needed the next dose of stimulant, and he hoped the descent would take less than that. If it didn't, at least he'd be too busy falling and dying to notice.

CHAPTER SIXTEEN

Ruby woke up with only one thought in her mind, that she needed to move fast. Based on what she'd learned two nights prior, much more was going on in Magic City than she'd ever imagined. She'd wanted to see Margrave the day before, but her family had come up with things for her to do at Spirits, and she had no justifiable reason to decline. Now, she was determined to get out of the house before anyone was awake to stop her. Idryll rose as she dressed and asked, "Want me to come along?"

Ruby shook her head. "I don't think I'm ready to introduce you to Margrave. He's certainly more than open-minded, but dealing with that in addition to the things I'm going to ask him for might push him right over the edge."

The tiger-woman yawned, stretched, and burrowed under the covers. "Fine with me. As long as someone brings food. There will be dire consequences if no one brings food."

Ruby laughed. "Yes, arms getting bitten off. I've heard.

Matthias is aware you're in here. I'm sure a dish of meat will arrive before you succumb to starvation."

"When do you think you'll introduce me to your family?" The question didn't carry any irritation or offense, as near as she could tell.

"I don't know that I will. Certainly not anytime soon, since the damn *venamisha* magic won't let me."

The other woman laughed. "There is that. I'm sure it's for your protection, somehow."

"Yeah, getting a little tired of putting up with things that are allegedly for my good, thanks." She finished dressing in her standard outfit of boots, jeans, and a t-shirt, plus her leather jacket. She circled her arms in a quick move to open a rift, then stepped through to the spot she'd found during her last visit to Vagrant's Crossing. As she let the magic opening fall closed behind her, she said, "That's much better than having to drive." She headed around the corner and crossed the road to her mentor's house. The animatronics on the lawn waved at her as she passed, bringing a smile to her face that widened as the man himself opened the door. She called, "How did you know I was coming?"

"Surveillance systems. Saw you when you walked out onto my street." She figured that he also knew her well enough to guess she'd come as early as reasonable after setting up the meet the day before. She followed him downstairs to the basement, and he gestured her toward the same chair she'd occupied on her last visit. The long worktable was empty, and the shelves were far neater than usual.

She asked, "Hosting other visitors?"

He shook his head. "No, I have this feeling that things will be busy for a while, and wanted to be sure everything was in its place."

"I can totally understand that. I did it at the start of the semester in my lab at school. And every break, now that I think about it. Compared to you though, my work area was chaos."

He laughed. "After the first decade, you start to get a sense of where you need things to be. You'll get there, don't worry. Now, you were quite mysterious on the phone about what you needed." He raised his hand and wiggled his fingers as if to illustrate the mystery. "What can I do for you?"

Ruby had been thinking hard about how much to tell him. She figured her connection to him wasn't well enough known to put him in danger, which would make it easier to share more of the truth. Still, this was new territory, and she was decidedly paranoid about sharing. On the other hand, he was more knowledgeable about both magical and mundane technology than she was, and if given the bigger picture, might come up with ideas she wouldn't. She waited a moment to see if her mental voice would chime in with a warning, and when it didn't, gave a little nod. "Okay. Here's the thing. I'm not sure if you're aware, but there's a lot of bad stuff going on in Ely."

He sat up straighter and crossed his arms, narrowing his gaze at her. "Yeah, I've heard. Coincidentally, it seemed to start when you got back to town, right?"

She shook her head. "That's what I thought, too. Turns out there's been a bunch of questionable things happening all along that I never saw. It doesn't make the papers, but the rumor mill is full of information about it. Con artists, gangs, a black market in magic items. Plus all the incidents you've heard about."

He gave a low whistle. "So, that's some deep trouble you've gotten into the middle of. What's it have to do with me?"

"I'm not going to stay on the sidelines. I need some magic tech, or even standard tech, to help me along."

He frowned. "What are you planning to do?"

She shrugged. "Whatever I can. I was in the building when those explosions killed people who didn't deserve to die. I can't let that go, and I have the ability to maybe help make a change."

He shook his head, perhaps unconsciously. "Sounds dangerous, Ruby. We have police and stuff for that kind of thing."

She barked a laugh. "The Magic City PD is spread too thin, and that's assuming they're not on the take, or whatever it's called on the cop shows. Sheriff Alejo is good people, but she has hardly any support. Plus, it appears magicals are involved, and Ely is way too small to have the sort of authorities required to defeat strong spellcasters."

"You think you can make a difference?" She heard his worry in the question.

"I'm sure I can. Plus, I'm sure I can do it in a way that there's only moderate danger to me and none to those I care about. However, I'm going to need every edge I can get."

Margrave sighed. "Well, Red," he used the nickname that he'd applied to her in high school, "I know you well enough to know you'll do it regardless of whether I agree.

So, if the choice is watching you go it alone or figuring out how to help you, of course I'll help. What do you need?"

She pushed down the surge of emotion that threatened her composure. "Thank you. Seriously." They talked about her potential needs for the next hour. Then they worked together for two more, building the items out of components he had in his shop. The simplest thing was a periscope, expandable and flexible so she could look around corners and over edges without a problem.

Next up was locators. He had created similar items for other clients and had the parts lying around. Much like the systems that allowed people to find their keys with their smartphones, these would send out a small ping at intervals to show where they were. He gave her five mundane versions and a receiver. Then, in case she needed to track someone where technology wouldn't work, like in the kemana, he provided a handful that radiated a certain kind of magic signal. It was sound-based, at a low frequency most beings wouldn't hear, human or magical. They practiced until she could find it with her magic, a process of attunement that took only a short time.

For communication, he offered encrypted walkie-talkies with earpieces, consumer-grade technology that he promised to upgrade with magic components if she found she needed it. He handed over her shield pendant, which he'd arranged to have recharged by one of his contacts. He said, "Okay, two more things, both more defensive than strictly useful. First, do you have access to potions?"

"I have a few stockpiled that I've gotten from Keshalla in the past. I can get more from her, I'm sure."

"If you need someone on this planet to provide them, I could probably set that up for you. Let me know."

She nodded. "Will do. What's the other thing?"

He went to the shelves and took down a small wooden box and placed it on the table before her. Opening the lid revealed four glass bulbs, each resembling an hourglass in the way it was divided into two separate parts, top and bottom. He said, "This is for escape, at need. When it meets the air, the chemical in the top will turn into smoke, quite a lot of it. The bottom contains glitter essentially, but a special kind of glitter that disrupts magic. Anyone trying to use magical senses to see through the smoke will find this blocks their ability to do so."

"Wow, really? What spell is that based on?"

"A blend of magic detection and illusion. Basically, it senses incoming magic and sends it back in reverse. It's not powerful enough to counteract an aggressive spell, like force or electricity. But the more subtle ones, like sensing, or tracking, it should work fine. We've only tested it a little."

"Who are you making it for?"

He chuckled. "That would be telling, and you know I can't do that. Suffice to say that it's for people with some authority."

"Speaking of which, I met someone with some authority recently. An agent with some government group. She seemed pretty sharp."

Margrave grinned. "Always good to have friends. Maybe you can get me a government contract." He rubbed his hands together. "That's where the real money is."

She laughed. "Thank you, Margrave. Seriously. You're a literal lifesaver."

He nodded. "I'm happy to help. Now, I'm sure you have better things to do than hang out with an old man, and I *do* have some work to complete for actual paying clients." It was a joke between them, and they were both fully aware that his only concerns about money were that he had enough to live on and continue his work.

She stood and collected the stuff. "If you think of any more clever ideas, I can put them to good use."

He rose to escort her out. "Just make sure you stay safe and healthy so that you can."

"Promise." *If anyone's going to wind up hurt, it's gonna be the bastards playing games in my city.*

CHAPTER SEVENTEEN

Her next destination was the Drow's shop in the kemana. She stepped cautiously through the door and stopped inside, nodding respectfully to the proprietor. "Greetings, Shentia."

The Drow nodded. She wore a simple dress today, in black, and her ashen hair was woven into a complicated braid that hung down over her shoulder. "Same to you. Have you decided to take me up on my invitation to examine my inventory?"

Ruby shook her head. "As much as I wish that was my reason for visiting today, I'm afraid it isn't. Instead, I'm hoping for some specific items. Back room kinds of items."

The other woman lifted an eyebrow questioningly. "Are you? I see. Well then, let's take a wander into the back." She led the way, and Ruby followed her into the rear of the shop. The Drow stopped in the middle and turned to her. "So, specifically, what are your needs?"

"I'm looking for weapons that work against magic

defenses and things I can use to defend against magic attacks."

"Indeed." She stared for several uncomfortable seconds, as if trying to judge why Ruby might need such things, then gave a brisk nod. "I happen to have three items that may help." She turned to the corner that held blades in individual racks. One of them displayed a pair of throwing knives: thin, sharp, and shining in silver with etchings all along them. Shentia lifted them from their holders and set them on her palm, then extended them for Ruby to examine.

"They're gorgeous. Drow-made?"

She nodded. "Indeed. Most people don't recognize such things right away."

Ruby chuckled. "My mentor Keshalla considers Drow weapons to be among the best."

"Intelligent person, then. They're exceedingly high quality. More than that though, they're imbued with magic that allows them to pierce magical defenses."

Ruby felt her eyes widen in surprise. "Like, go through a force shield?"

"Exactly."

"Wow. I've never heard of such a thing. Wonderful."

The Drow nodded and set them aside to pick up a short dagger. The pommel was no bigger than her fist, and the blade about half again that size. "This isn't an artifact weapon, but nonetheless has one of the properties of arti-fact weapons, in that you can cast magic through it."

Ruby had read a great deal about artifact weapons in her studies at the university. One of those would be virtu-ally priceless. This dagger would allow her to use it for physical defense while not compromising her ability to cast spells, which would be amazing. "Excellent. I would love to have that, as well."

The Drow nodded. "Very good." She moved to the opposite side of the room, where mannequin pieces held worn items. A pair of arms stuck up from the shelf, each with a bracer attached to it. They were in the form of thick black tooled leather cuffs. Each had three rings of a silver metal running around it, with different etching than the trio of blades had.

Ruby wasn't sure if these were of Drow manufacture or not, so she kept her mouth shut about their provenance. "What do they do?"

"Striking them together will create a magic shield that will sustain itself for fifteen seconds or so. They have three charges, represented by the bands, but afterward must be fully replenished before you can use them again."

Ruby knew a great deal about the need to store power into magic items that spent it, a problem shared by all magic tech items and most magical items other than artifacts and artifact weapons. "I'll take those as well."

The other woman smiled. "There is the matter of payment."

Ruby replied, "Of course. How much?" The Drow named a number that left her speechless with shock. If she drained all her accounts, she would have enough to pay for it but no money to start her business. While she could borrow from her family, she had no desire to put herself in that situation.

Shentia chuckled. "That is more often than not the reaction I get when I mention how much magical items cost. Usually, I deal with the representatives of collectors, though, and they go back and talk to their principals, and eventually they come to a number at least close to the one I suggest. However, in your case, I have a different idea. I would be willing to lend these items to you free of charge, in exchange for a favor at a later date."

Ruby remembered Diana's caution and was well aware that the Drow was deliberately putting her in her debt. *There's not much I can do about it unless I want to give up all my money, and these are too important not to have.* "I accept, but I won't do anything against my principles. That must be part of the agreement."

The Drow shrugged. "I'm sure we can find something appropriate."

Ruby replied, "Done."

Shentia nodded. "Done." She paused, then continued, "I would hesitate to assume anything, but based upon your selections, one imagines that whatever you require these for might also necessitate a disguise."

In for a penny, in for a pound. "Two of them."

Her host gestured toward a third section of the room, where mannequin heads wore various pieces of jewelry and ornamental masks. "These are magic items that will change according to the user's will once donned. Should the magic be penetrated, the physical covering still protects the wearer's identity."

They looked vaguely like kabuki masks, white porcelain with no particular expression. The object covered the entire face except for the mouth and swept back to cover the ears and latch behind the head. She touched one and discovered it was a pliant material, rather than something resistant, despite its looks. They would be perfect, at least for the near term.

Ruby asked, "These can be part of our current arrangement?"

Shentia nodded but clarified, "Since you're likely going into danger, we must make a further agreement that if any item is destroyed or lost, additional compensation will be required."

"Of course. That's only fair."

For the first time during the visit, the Drow broke into a full smile. "Very good. I look forward to a long and fruitful partnership, Ruby Achera."

Ruby walked the short distance back to her family's house, pondering the decisions she'd made. Everything seemed to be going more or less smoothly, although she feared to think what the favor she owed the Drow might turn out to be. Ultimately, though, that didn't matter. She'd continue to do what she must to protect the people in her city. As soon as she was inside, her sister intercepted her. "Did you hear?"

"Hear what?"

"About the attack. Well, actually, attacks."

Ruby's anxiety surged at the question. "No, I haven't. What's going on?"

Morrigan replied, "How about some tea?" It was old code for finding a private place to talk, which often turned out to be the small table in the kitchen, as long as the staff wasn't using it. They waved to the cook as they entered, and he pointed them to the table without them needing to ask. A pot of tea and a plate of cookies appeared a few moments later as if by magic, although actually by the efforts of another staff member, and Ruby nibbled one as her sister launched into an explanation.

"So, all the casino owners have been talking about the latest one. Somebody broke into Deep Woods and killed Lachsan. They tried to kill Enelle but only injured her. She's in the hospital. Tryn knocked the attacker out a window while the intruder was focused on trying to kill his mother."

Ruby shivered from her neck down to her toes. "That's horrible. Did they catch whoever did it?"

Morrigan shook her head. "He got away. At least they presume it was a he. The intruder disabled the cameras on the way to the secure area, and the staff on those floors only saw a person in a mask. Everyone's saying they moved like a man, although how they know exactly how a man moves, I have no idea."

"I think people who spend their lives fighting, martial artists and such, get some intuition about that. Maybe that's how. What's the other?"

Her sister replied, "I heard about this one from one of our security people, who was discussing it with another one."

Ruby gave a fake frown. "Eavesdropping again?"

"I prefer the term information gathering. In any case, he said there was an attack on another security company."

She kept her voice steady as she asked, "Like the other one, some kind of break-in?"

Her sister shook her head. "From the sound of it, it was

a full-on attack. They killed people, and they burned down the building."

"Ouch." She drummed her fingers, thinking. "Any idea of a motive? Any connections?"

Morrigan shrugged. "They didn't say. I looked the company up on the Internet before I came back down and found out they were the ones in charge of security for the Kraken and The Hunt."

Ruby frowned. "So, that's two attacks on the Atlanteans. And a kid involved in both the Atlantean one and the Wood Elf one. Still, nothing really connects the one at Mist or the one at the Ebon Dragon." *Except, of course, Aces Security was behind the kidnapping attempt and the move on the Dragon. I wonder if they had anything to do with either of these others.*

Morrigan nodded. "It's frustrating, not knowing what's going on. Speaking of which, what exactly are *you* up to?"

Ruby's mind went into lockdown for a moment, surprised by the question. Then she shook her head and replied, "It's best if no one knows. That way no one's in danger."

"So there *is* something. I knew it. You'll need help."

She chuckled. "Oh, trust me, I have all the help I need."

Her sister looked confused. "What do you mean?"

Ruby waved a hand. "Can't explain. Would if I could. Now, I think I need to find out more about what's going on."

Morrigan touched her hand. "Promise me something."

Her seriousness stopped Ruby halfway out of her chair, and she sat again. "If I can."

"I get that you think some things have to be secret. Tell

me whatever you can. Share information. I might see patterns or connections that you don't since I know and talk to different people. I don't have to seek news the way you might because it's constantly flowing around me. Still, I won't know what matters unless you keep me in the loop."

She considered the request. Truly, what her sister said was correct, and sharing some things wouldn't bring her into any extra danger. "Okay. Done."

She headed to her room for a quick shower and a change of clothes, then portaled up to the garage near her surface house. She wandered inside, greeted her roommates, then knocked on Demetrius's door. He called, "Come in," and she did. He was in his usual spot, seated at his keyboard with three curved monitors in a semi-circle before him. She never understood most of what she saw on those displays; it was a blend of technology and magic that seemed almost alive in the way that it was constantly moving. The technologist inside her was interested, but she had other things demanding her attention.

She asked, "Do you have time to take on a gig?"

He shrugged and swiveled his chair away from the monitors to face her. "Maybe. Depends on what it is."

"I want you to collect as much data about criminal activity in town as you can."

"Wouldn't be too hard. Public-sector databases, mostly, and they rarely have the strongest defenses. Why?"

She kept her expression blank to hide her slight deception. "It's for my family. They'll pay your normal rate, no problem."

He chuckled. "Corporate espionage?"

She shook her head. "More like self-defense. You heard about the attack on Deep Woods, right?"

"Yeah. That sucks."

"It does. That's why we need all the information we can get. I'm not sure if all the threads are being examined as a whole, or if Ely PD is looking at local crime, and the sheriff is looking at bigger stuff, and the Paranormal Defense Agency a whole set of other things. I need someone who can pull that all together."

He nodded. "Okay. I'm in. I should be able to have most of the raw data by tomorrow if I work overnight."

She stepped over and patted him on the shoulder. "You're the best. And I'm not saying that in hopes of a discount."

Demetrius grinned and barked a laugh. "Good, because I don't do discounts, not even for friends."

She waved as she departed, then hustled to her room, locked the door, and opened a portal back to her bedroom in the kemana. It took only a moment for Idryll to step through, and Ruby let the opening close. She pulled clothes from the dresser for the shapeshifter, then veiled her and led her out of the house, not stopping to talk with anyone. Once they were outside, they headed for the garage so she could create another portal. Idryll asked, "Where are we going?"

"I have one more thing I need to put in place before we can really get started. We need an emergency hideout, and I know just the spot." She created a portal to the bottom of the hill and sighed at the long climb leading to the abbey. A quick burst of magic transformed the tiger woman into a normal-looking human, and they walked up to the building at the top. A request to speak with the Abbot resulted in an escort to the man's office, located in a part of the abbey Ruby hadn't yet seen. He rose from behind his desk and smiled, extending a hand to shake both of theirs. "Ruby, so good to see you again. Who's your friend?"

"This is Idryll. Idryll, Abbott Thomas."

Her partner said, "A pleasure. This is an amazing place you have."

He nodded with a proud smile. "It's astonishing what a group of like-minded people can accomplish, given enough time and motivation." He gestured them to seats across his desk and returned to his own. "Now, what can I do for you?"

Ruby asked, "Before, you mentioned that if someone sought sanctuary here, you would provide it. I wondered if that would extend to actively helping people in danger, or people who were injured."

A concerned frown replaced his smile. "Of course. That's the very essence of providing sanctuary, aiding those in need."

Ruby nodded. "I had to ask. Idryll, you can show him." Ruby let her illusion fall, hoping her words would lead the Abbott to conclude that her partner was the one who'd created it. His eyes widened at the sight of her in her tiger-woman form, then he smiled.

"You're beautiful. I especially like the colors in your hair."

Idryll replied with a smile, "Thank you. I am pleased you're not frightened or shocked at my appearance."

Abbott Thomas shook his head. "We've seen many kinds here, and welcome all."

Ruby asked, "Do you have a place we could portal to in an emergency? Somewhere out of the way, where anyone visiting won't see?"

He rose and gestured toward the door. "Yes."

"You're fine with us using this? It wouldn't be except as a last resort, to get innocents out of trouble. I promise we won't abuse the privilege."

He nodded as he led them down a short hallway and showed them an empty room. "Of course. Totally fine. We'll put a bell in here so that anyone who comes in can ring for help."

Ruby felt a weight lift from her shoulders. "Great. Do you have a healer here?"

"We have people with medical training, and we can always call for help. You can count on us, Ruby. We'll take care of anyone you feel the need to place into our hands."

"Thank you, Abbott Thomas. I'll find a way to repay you."

He laughed. "No matter. If there's a reason we exist, helping people in times of need is it."

Ruby and Idryll wandered slowly back down the hill, side by side. The tiger woman asked, "So, are we ready?"

Ruby nodded. "Definitely. Tomorrow, we start putting the pieces together and seeing where they lead."

CHAPTER EIGHTEEN

Demetrius was as good as his word, and by the next morning, Ruby had a memory stick with all the data he could find. She called the number Diana had given her and was surprised when someone different answered. A female voice said, "Ruby?"

"Yeah, who is this?" As an afterthought, "How did you know it was me?"

The person on the other end of the line laughed. "Well, first, caller ID. Also, when the boss hands out cards, the numbers are unique, so this number will always be you. I'm Glam, or Kayleigh, whichever you prefer."

"Yeah, then, this is Ruby, obviously." She paused for a second to get her mouth to stop leading her brain. "I have some data I was wondering if you could take a look at, maybe help me sort through."

"Oh, I think that's something we can do. Hang on a sec." The line was silent for half a minute, then her voice returned. "The boss says she'll pick you up outside the

Drow's shop, whatever that means, in a half-hour. She'll bring you over here, and we'll work on what you have."

"Perfect." She said her goodbyes and headed for the meet. A half-hour later, she stepped through the portal into the agents' secret base. They arrived in a room that seemed like it was designed specifically for that purpose, based on the lack of furniture. It was all metal and strange shapes and looked like something that would have been a perfect set for a science fiction movie.

Diana apologized and left for a meeting. Rath escorted Ruby into a highly technological workspace. Brightly lit, clean, with lots of metal and plastic, it was the sort of workshop she could appreciate. A woman with blonde curls that fell below her shoulders popped up from a desk in the corner and said with a smile, "You have to be Ruby, obviously. I'm Kayleigh. Over there is Deacon." She raised her voice and called, "Deacon, say hello." The man in the office to their right lifted a hand and obediently shouted, "Hello," then went back to his computers.

The other woman waved her forward to a set of monitors mounted along one wall. "You said you had some data?"

Ruby nodded and held out the memory stick. "One of my roommates is a really good infomancer."

"Excellent. Always good to have extra people around to carry the load, right? Even Deacon and I find it challenging on occasion to handle all the investigation we're asked to do."

Kayleigh sat at the keyboard in front of the monitors and called up the data. "Okay, pretty standard stuff, database of locations and events, categorized. I can work with that." She tapped the keys, and a map appeared on the biggest monitor and started to populate with markers in various colors. Text boxes materialized beside them and filled in the details. A robbery here, a break-in there, plus the big events marked in bright red. Each icon glowed with a different intensity, and it only took her a moment to realize it was a reference to the timeline, and more recent things were brighter. Once new data stopped popping onto the map, Kayleigh said, "Okay, we have a good baseline here. Now, what specific information are you looking for?"

"There's a black market in magic items going on in town, as you know, at least partly located in pawnshops. Since the same person owns several of these businesses, I wondered if there might be a distribution point or something like that. Somewhere that stuff from out of town lands before they put it out into the individual locations."

Kayleigh looked back over her shoulder with a frown. "That's a bit of a leap, at least based on this data. Why do you think it exists?"

"I guess it's instinct. Maybe I heard something I'm not consciously aware of. It feels like a strong possibility."

The tech turned to her computer and drummed her fingers on the desk for a moment. "Okay, if a storage location does exist, we can assume there would be repeated traffic between that site and the pawnshops in question. I don't suppose you know which ones they are?"

Ruby replied, "Only one."

Kayleigh gave a small snort. "Never mind then, that wouldn't be useful." She picked up a headset and put it on. "Deacon?" She paused, then continued, "I need access to all the traffic cam records for Ely, Nevada. Say, for the last month." She paused again, clearly listening, then said, "Now, of course." Another pause, this one accompanied by a shake of her head. "No, I don't care if you're in the middle of an arena battle, do it."

After a few minutes, the data she wanted appeared, and she set the machine to analysis. Lines began to draw on the display, paths from place to place by vehicles, the tech explained. They watched as tracks covered the image, then she hit some buttons and only the thickest ones, representing the frequently taken routes, remained. When she highlighted the pawnshops, it became clear that a path connected a bunch of them back to the same small warehouse at the edge of town. Kayleigh laughed. "Well, look at that. If there is one, that's the spot."

The other computer wrangler wandered in at that point, apparently having finished whatever game he was playing. Kayleigh surrendered her seat, waved at him to take her place, and asked, "Can you whip up some real-time satellite on that place?"

He shook his head. "You say that like it doesn't involve hacking a national security satellite to do it."

Kayleigh looked at Ruby and rolled her eyes. "Come on, don't complain. You know you love messing with the government."

He laughed. "She's not wrong." A few moments later they got an image showing a warehouse in an industrial area surrounded by several similar constructions. The top-down angle wasn't particularly useful, and the tech accessed Google Street View to show more views of the spot.

Rath commented, "You should learn how to fly. You could land on the roof from one of those nearby buildings."

Ruby laughed. "I'll get right on that. Know anyone who can teach me?"

"I can fly. I have a flight suit."

She blinked. "Really?"

Kayleigh replied, "Yep. He flies really well. It's basically a box with retractable wings and a harness. More glider than anything, but he has great body control and can make it work almost like it was under power."

Ruby smiled down at him. "Well, okay. I'll put that on my to-do list, and maybe you can teach me."

He nodded with a grin. "Will. Fun."

Kayleigh said, "So, I imagine you're going to take a look at this place in person, is that right?"

"Yeah. I'm not happy about what's happening in town, and it wouldn't surprise me at all if the people who were behind the black market had a role in the other stuff as well."

The tech crossed to her work area in the corner and pulled a small box off the shelf. She turned and set it on one of the room's plastic-covered tables. She opened it to reveal an earpiece tiny enough to fit completely inside her ear. "The boss is giving you access to our comms system. You won't be able to hear our communications unless we want you to, but you can call us with it at any time. Deacon and I will give you a hand if you need computer or technical support while you're in the field, assuming we're not already on some other task."

She handed over the device, and Ruby turned it over in her hands. "It'll connect all the way to here?"

The tech nodded. "We piggyback on some other stuff, but yeah, there's really nowhere you can go on the planet that we won't be able to connect with you. Well, except maybe New Atlantis."

Ruby laughed. "I don't think I'm set for an ocean vacation anytime soon. They don't exactly encourage tourists."

Kayleigh nodded. "That, they do not." She closed the box and returned it to the shelf. Turning back, she said, "If you use the code word Aries, that'll be essentially a nine-one-one call to us. Whoever we have available will come in force to help you. If we do, we'll all probably wind up on the PDA's radar. It seems like they're taking quite an interest in the goings-on in Magic City."

Ruby frowned. "You're the second person to tell me that in the last few days."

"They're not exactly subtle. We don't have any information on what their goal is, but those folks cast a wide net." Her scowl showed her opinion of their methods. "You'd be wise to keep an eye out for them."

"Will do."

Kayleigh grinned. "Well, I think we've done all we can do for you. You have a half-hour or so before Diana gets back, and I know she'd like to say goodbye. So, Rath, how about you give her a tour?"

The troll swept up in a somersault. "First stop, come meet Max."

That night found Ruby and Idryll fully outfitted and ready to go. They were in matching clothes consisting of black boots, black tactical pants, black long sleeve shirts, black jackets, and the white masks Shentia had provided. Her partner wasn't thrilled with wearing the outfit but agreed it made sense to do so, at least for now. Ruby guessed the tiger woman would eventually abandon the disguise, but that was something they'd have to figure out once they got there. In truth, as long as they didn't appear in public both out of disguise, it wouldn't matter if anyone saw her. Still, it felt like keeping things under wraps for the moment was a good idea.

She had the toys Margrave had provided strapped onto a wide belt, except for the potions, which she'd hidden in her thigh pockets. The throwing knives were stuck in the belt, too; she hadn't had a chance to come up with a better solution. The dagger was in a sheath at her hip, and she carried her sword in a scabbard on her back. She would coat it with force magic to turn it into a blunt object when battle permitted, but she was prepared to do real damage if the situation required it.

They were crouched on a taller building across a small lane from the warehouse and had used the listening device to identify the opposition within. She knew several guards patrolled the structure, both on the bottom floor and on what was at least a catwalk, to judge by the ringing sound it made, or possibly a whole upper level with a metal surface. She pointed at a fire escape that ended at a door on the second floor. "I think that's our entrance."

Idryll nodded. "Works for me. Take out the ones on the top quietly, then go after the rest?"

"Excellent plan. Do your best not to kill anybody, but if it's them or us, then it's us. Assuming they're armed or whatever." She could never quite get a handle on her partner's threshold for serious violence but figured the tiger-woman generally reached it much faster than Ruby hit hers.

"Don't worry about me. Just keep yourself alive while we're working on opposite sides."

"You know it. Okay. Let's do this."

CHAPTER NINETEEN

Ruby created a force slide, inwardly cursing her inability to simply portal to a spot she could easily see, and she and Idryll slid over to the fire escape. They landed with a light clatter and froze in place, waiting to find out if anyone discovered them. When no response came, Ruby tried the handle and found it locked. She stepped aside, and the tiger-woman extended a claw and raked it down through the small opening between door and jamb. Fortunately, the warehouse's defenses weren't high tech, and the barrier popped free. Ruby pulled it open enough for her partner to slip through and followed her in.

It was a catwalk, but twice as wide as a normal one, with boxes scattered here and there. It ran around the entire rectangular skin of the warehouse, with a metal ladder descending at about the midway point on each side. This level was poorly lit, only some dim lamps hanging from the ceiling. Below, the main floor was awash in light from fixtures on the walls, and loud conversations echoed through the space as a handful of men opened crates and moved boxes.

Idryll had gone to the left, so Ruby crept to her right, staying low and being as quiet as possible. If she'd been in charge of the building's defenses, the guards on the catwalk would be walking a rotation. Instead, each was looking down at the first floor, the notion that someone might come in from above clearly never having entered their defensive plans. *One more thing for the list, something to knock people out quietly without killing them.* Lacking such an option, she crept until she was about five feet away from the man who leaned on the railing, his forearms resting on it as he bent to look below.

She moved forward in a rush, reached out to put her hand over his mouth, and wrenched him backward with it. He slammed into the back wall with a muted *clang*, and she stepped across and delivered a right hook to his temple. She caught him as he went down and lowered him gently to the metal floor. *Thank heaven these morons have their weapons holstered.* The man's rifle was on a strap, but if he'd been holding a pistol, there's no way it wouldn't have fallen and given her away. She disarmed him and hid the weapons behind some nearby boxes, then peered over at where Idryll had gone and saw the guard from that side had vanished. Now the challenge would be getting to the remaining two before they noticed their friends had disappeared. Ruby called up a veil and moved quickly, confident after taking a quick look at the downed guard's gear that the criminals didn't have magic detectors.

Her target's head whipped around at a clatter from across the room, and Ruby was still too far away to cover his mouth. She reflexively blasted him with lightning, hoping to lock up his muscles and keep him quiet. The noise from below masked the crackling sound and the first part of the plan went off perfectly as her target stiffened but didn't shout. Part two, where she got close and took him down quietly, wasn't quite as perfect. The man leaned to his left, balanced on the railing for a minute, and tipped over. It was almost like watching a slow-motion action movie, how his tumbling body moved through space on the way down. When he crashed into a low stack of boxes at the bottom, things snapped back into full speed as shouts and gunshots rang out.

Ruby put one hand on the railing and leapt over it, dropping fast and blunting her impact with a burst of force magic. She landed right beside a human with a wicked scar across his forehead. He pointed his weapon at her with an impressive lack of shock, and she slapped it away before he could pull the trigger. His response was swift, a quick jab from his offhand that caught her in the shoulder as she ducked away to protect her face. She flashed out a double punch, both fists connecting simultaneously with his chest and causing him to stumble backward. As she charged in with a follow-up, he planted his foot and snapped out a kick, forcing her to abandon her attack and curve off to the side. The new angle showed her more of the building's first floor, and she realized more enemies were present than she'd thought.

Idryll was a whirl of motion across the way, occupying a couple of the black market warehouse workers. However, at least six more remained and guns were coming out in everybody's hands, which meant she had no time to delay.

Ruby whipped the sword from her back, wrapped it in force magic, and slashed out at her opponent with all her strength. It caught him with a heavy blow on the chest, and bones cracked as he flew backward. She charged toward the next, calling up a force shield in her left hand to block the bullets firing at her. Even as a blunt instrument, her sword was a devastating weapon. She swiped across to knock the man's gun out of his hand by shattering his wrist, then hacked it down to smash into his knee, destroying the joint. He fell with a scream, and she kicked his pistol away as she positioned herself to face her next enemy.

The man fired a pair of pistols at her, seizing the triggers in an almost convulsive fashion. She'd tried to use two simultaneously at the range once, to see what it was like, and had been unable to hit with either of them. Her foe had the same problem. She dashed at him and jumped in the air, snapping out a front kick that connected with his forearms as he frantically tried to block his face. She landed and spun, delivering a sidekick to his sternum that dropped him gasping to the floor. Ahead, a door slammed open as one of the three remaining bad guys fled. She called, "Get him, kitty cat."

Idryll's voice floated back as she dashed in pursuit. "Don't call me kitty cat."

Ruby grinned as she stalked toward the two hoodlums left standing. This pair had gotten smart and were far enough apart that she couldn't engage both of them at once with her weapon or her fists. She summoned a force shield to intercept the oncoming bullets, sheathed her sword in a swift motion, and reached out with a line of force to snag a nearby wooden crate. She whipped her arm forward and threw the container at the one on the right, and he had only enough time to screech in fear before it leveled him. Ruby walked calmly toward the remaining foe, holding her shield in front of her as she approached. He fired the gun dry, then fumbled to replace the magazine.

At that moment, she let her shield go, stepped forward, and knocked the weapon out of his hand with an open-handed slap. She stopped, staring at him. He'd see the illusion of a cat's face, a little touch that her partner had approved. The man threw a punch, and she blocked it easily. He tried for a kick, and she stopped that, too. Then she imagined invisible bands covering his body, and her force magic reached out to make it a reality. He stiffened, arms dropped at his side, then fell. She caught him before his head struck the floor and laid him gently down.

A clatter from the doorway came as Idryll returned and threw the man she was dragging halfway across the room. He hit the cement floor hard and screeched. From the strange angle of his arm, it was clear that at least one bone had snapped, either before or after his short flight.

Ruby shook her head. "You broke him. What if we needed to have a conversation?"

Her partner snorted. "First, if you want prisoners, say so. Second, this one is too stupid to know anything. He tried to hide behind a bush. From me. I mean, that wouldn't work against anyone, but against me? Downright insulting."

Ruby chuckled. "Well, I guess he got what he deserved, then. Fortunately, I have one for us to talk to." A door led into an office area, which was doubtless where the extra bad guys had come from, and she used force magic to drag the bound prisoner in that direction. "Make sure none of these jerks can leave, ideally without hurting them more. I saw some rope over there in the corner. I'll get this guy ready, and we'll have a conversation."

Ruby had put the man in a chair and tied him with some extension cords she'd found so she wouldn't have to maintain the flow of magic. She pushed the chair back against the wall so he couldn't hurl himself backward and break his head and sat on the edge of the beat-up metal desk that was the room's only other furniture. When Idryll returned, she stood in the doorway with her arms crossed, looking menacing.

They went quickly through the preliminaries, with the man refusing to share any useful information. He swore and threatened and was generally unhelpful. That lasted right up until the moment Idryll stomped forward, extended a single claw, and showed it to him before using it to slice a shallow furrow in his face. After that demonstration, he was far more willing to answer.

Ruby asked, "Who's in charge of your operation?"

He was sweating with pain or fear, and his voice trembled. "We work for the dwarf. Tarrant."

"Is he the top of the food chain?"

The man shook his head. "Don't know. I doubt it. He's not so smart."

"What is this place?"

"What does it look like?" Idryll shifted her weight

toward him, and his sudden display of attitude vanished back into fear. "It's a warehouse. Stuff comes in, and we uncrate it, or we put things together to go somewhere else. Not too often. Supposed to be a shipment tonight, but it didn't come."

They asked several more questions, trying to glean information about Tarrant's operation, the pawnshop break-in, plus the casino and security company attacks, but the man was useless. Finally, Ruby gave up in frustration although she masked it from their captive. "Okay, I think we've had enough from him. Let's call in the sheriff."

The man looked panicked. "No, you can't. They'll know I talked to you. You have to hurt me some more, or maybe just make it look like you did, or the boss will get more suspicious."

Ruby exchanged glances with Idryll, who had also caught the comment. She replied, "*More* suspicious? If there's something you're not telling us, you'd better fix that right now, or we'll make sure everyone outside knows that you spilled."

Any remaining resilience the man possessed ran out of him in a rush. "I've been dealing on the side. An expensive item disappeared recently, and the boss, or his boss, or *someone* noticed. They've been sniffing around. Asking questions."

"Who did you sell it to?"

"Don't know. The buyer used a drone. Sent the money, I checked it; then I sent the case with the items in it. No way of knowing who it was."

Drones are one of those areas where technology causes as many problems as it solves. She asked, "Okay, what was it?"

"Armor. Technology and magic, I think. It was apparently really rare. I got a good price for it." The last was said almost as a justification.

Ruby shook her head. "I'd suggest when you get out of prison, that you find a new line of work. You're definitely not smart enough for this one." She led Idryll outside. "I think it's time for you to go home. I need to call the sheriff and have a chat with her."

She expected an argument, but one didn't come. After her partner was home, she pulled the burner phone she'd taken to carrying when she couldn't use hers from her belt, turned it on, and called the sheriff's office to report a crime.

CHAPTER TWENTY

After making the call, Ruby collected all the fallen hoodlums and gathered them in the center of the room,
ensuring they were all securely tied together. She protected
the ones with broken or damaged limbs with force splints
while she moved them, but she couldn't feel too badly
about it. She and Idryll hadn't killed anyone, and she was
certain they wouldn't have returned that favor if things
had gone their way. She also grabbed a canvas bag lying in
a corner and filled it with the objects that looked most
valuable. She imagined they would sit in an evidence
locker for years and doubted their owners would want to
wait for them that long. *Plus, if we can't figure out who owns
them, maybe we can sell them and donate the money or
something.*

When she heard sirens in the distance, she took her
collection and headed up to the catwalk. She opened a
portal and threw the bag into the bedroom at her parents'
house, then summoned a veil and hid in the corner. She
watched as the local police department and Sheriff Alejo

came in with guns raised and made sure the danger had passed. This crime scene was much different than the one at the pawnshop. Technicians and officers worked methodically, clearing out the prisoners and taking inventory of what had transpired, looking for clues. More like the cop shows she'd seen, although still not quite the same.

She waited and watched, and finally, the sheriff went into a corner to take a phone call. Ruby carefully crossed so she was above her, and when Alejo clicked off, Ruby created a force magic tunnel to carry her whisper from the top floor to the bottom. The illusion changed her voice, making it sound older and harsher than it was. "Sheriff. Don't be alarmed. I'm about to come down to talk to you."

The other woman started, then looked around, including up. Ruby cast a different veil to separate the sheriff from the rest of the people on the bottom floor and dropped the one hiding her. She put one hand on the railing and vaulted over, using force magic to stop her fall.

Alejo took in the figure before her, doubtless wondering why she'd chosen to look like a humanoid cat. *Maybe someday you'll find out.* The sheriff's right hand rested on her holstered pistol. "Who are you?"

Ruby replied, "A friend."

"To me? Don't believe we've met."

She shook her head. "To the citizens of Ely. You as well. You can call me, uh, Leopard." *Way to go, Ruby. Show up in disguise without a good name. Might as well tell her who you really are since she'll probably figure out there's only one person she's met recently so desperately awkward as to forget they needed a secret name.*

The other woman nodded. "Okay, Leopard." She

managed not to make it sound ridiculous, which was a plus. "What are you doing here?"

Ruby shrugged. "Helping."

"Violating a ton of laws, more like. Breaking and entering, assault, battery, criminal mischief, we can go on."

She shook her head. "Things are getting bad in Magic City, Sheriff. You can't pretend you don't see it. Since magic is involved, I'm sorry to say that puts it out of your league, more or less."

Alejo frowned. "I have resources."

"I have no doubt you're using them to their greatest effect. That doesn't change things. Unless you get a sudden influx of personnel or tech, most magicals will have an edge. They won't have quite as much of one against me."

The other woman scowled. "I'd like to say that you're wrong. I'd like to be able to say that the law's sufficient. These days, it seems as if our corner of the world is getting weirder by the minute, so those statements would be lies."

She smiled encouragingly. "No argument here. So, I'll help."

Alejo nodded. "Let's get one thing clear, though. The moment you step out of line and hurt an innocent or something you do results in harm to someone who shouldn't be, I'll come for you without reservation. You don't have a mandate. You don't have permission. At best, you have a time in which I'll focus my energies elsewhere." She laughed darkly. "Heaven knows I have plenty of other things to focus on."

"Understood. I'll share information freely with you if you do the same."

The sheriff sighed. "Yes, sure, of course." At that

moment, Ruby realized how frustrated the other woman was, how close to being overwhelmed by her inability to solve the mysteries cropping up.

"So, what can you tell me about the Deep Woods?"

This laugh was starker still. "Not a damn thing, really. I managed a look at the crime scene, a couple of floors of blood and damage, and a bedroom with a chalk outline. That's all I got before the Paranormal Defense Agency took over, since, as you mentioned, magic was involved." Her eyes narrowed. "Was it you?"

Ruby shook her head and put as much honesty as she could into her voice. "Never."

Alejo stared at her, then nodded acknowledgment. "If you say so. Anyway, the mother is in a coma in the hospital, and the son is now running the casino. The family will never be the same. There's no reason for it, not that I can see."

"Me neither. Together, maybe we'll figure it out."

The other woman asked, "Why did you want to talk to me in particular?"

"First, because you're top of the food chain. Second, because there's nothing in your history that suggests you're anything other than honest, dedicated, and at need, pragmatic. I don't think anyone else on your force would've been as open-minded."

"So what you're saying is that I'm an easily manipulated idiot."

Ruby grinned. "That's certainly not how I would describe you. In any case, it's time for me to go because someone's coming to look for you."

The sheriff looked over her shoulder, then returned her gaze to Ruby. "How do I contact you?"

Ruby shook her head. "You don't. I'll contact you." She called in another veil, effectively banishing herself from the woman's vision, then made her way slowly to the exit. It wasn't a particularly dramatic departure, but the important thing was that no one noticed her.

If she'd looked up before rounding the corner and casting a portal to leave the area, she might've noticed the hooded figure that watched from a nearby building. As it was, that person also remained unnoticed.

Jared pulled his SUV into the garage at Aces Security and killed the engine with a growl. Although their last action had been a complete success, and their experts were right now digging through all the data they collected to ensure the other company would never be viable again, it didn't *feel* like a win. It was the news of the killing on that same night that made him feel that way, as if the boss was using his company as a diversion for something bigger. He didn't like the thought that he wasn't involved in the most important actions, not one bit.

He exited the car and slammed the door, an admittedly childish move that entirely failed to lessen his frustration. He stomped up the stairs to his office and had enough time to make himself a drink—double whiskey on the rocks—and sit behind his desk before his partner walked in. The dwarf said, "The thing at Deep Woods is irritating as hell."

Grentham dropped into the chair across the desk with a snarl of annoyance.

Jared nodded. "Right? I'm not sure if we got played or not, setting up our event for that night, but it sure seems like we did."

"It's that lunatic Goryo who's behind it. I'm sure of it."

"Me too. The real question is whether he did it on his own, or because the boss told him to."

His partner scowled. "Yeah, I've asked myself that a bunch of times. Can't come to a useful answer though, so I guess it doesn't matter. What's done is done. Still, if I see that guy, I'm going to put him down. I have no faith that he won't come after us, eventually."

"What would the boss say?" It wasn't a condemnation of the idea, not at all, only a consideration of the outcome.

The dwarf chuckled. "I'll burn the body so badly no one will ever know who did it. The boss might suspect, but there will be no evidence left to prove it. Trust me, I can make sure of it."

Jared didn't doubt that his partner could do what he'd said. "Let's consider that our last option, though. Maybe there's a way we can turn this to our advantage. Blame some things on him, that sort of thing."

The dwarf shrugged, and it didn't look like agreement. "Relatedly, how can we turn the thing at Deep Woods into a benefit?"

He replied, "Well, the kid has already put out a call for proposals to beef up security, so we'll put in a bid. I'll lowball it to see if we can get in there."

"Good, good. We're still going to have the company officially stay away from the Atlanteans for a while?"

Jared sighed. "As much as I don't want to, I think it's the right decision. Delayed gratification on that one." He sat up in his chair and leaned forward, his mouth twisting into a frown. "I have to tell you something though, in strictest confidence. Swear to me you won't breathe a word of it."

The dwarf matched his change in posture. "Sworn. Of course. What's up?"

"Up 'til now, I felt pretty good about the idea that the boss had long-term plans for us. That once he'd accomplished what he wanted to here in Ely, he'd move on to other things and leave us in charge. I've lost that faith, and now I wonder if he intends for us to be with him at the other end of all this."

Grentham nodded. "Have to admit; I've had the same thought. Think it's time we did something about it?"

"I do. Nothing huge, yet. Still, making sure we always have bodyguards with us, at least until the stuff all shakes out, might be a good idea."

The dwarf chuckled. "Might put a bit of a damper on your dating life."

Jared gave a crooked smile. "Yeah, I already thought of that, and I *still* think it's a good idea. That should tell you how concerned I am."

"It does. I agree. Bodyguards, lower profile, treat ourselves like principals in need of protection."

"Exactly. Glad we're agreed."

The dwarf said, "I already have a couple I can detail to myself. Do you want me to pick some for you?"

He nodded. "Yeah, please do. Make sure at least one of them is a magical since I'm not."

"You got it." The dwarf rose and headed for the door.

"I'll arrange it right now. I think this is a good idea. Oh, and we're still good for the other thing, right?"

"Of course. The boss told us to do it, so we have to do it. And do it *big*, so he decides we're worth keeping around."

Grentham grinned. "Perfect. I'm a huge fan of *big*. I'll make it happen. You focus on selling us to the elves."

The door closed behind him, and Jared nodded to himself. *Yeah, do it big. Because if the boss decides we're expendable, no amount of bodyguards can keep us safe for long.*

CHAPTER TWENTY-ONE

After a long nap to make up for spending the night before out on the streets, Ruby threw her finds in a backpack and headed out to Shentia's shop. She'd asked Idryll to stay behind, still not willing to share that connection unnecessarily. *So much hidden information to keep track of. It seems like I'm coming down with a bad case of the secrets as well.* She found the Drow sitting in her customary spot behind the counter in the front room and leaned on the display case that separated that section of the space from the entrance. "I have a question for you," she said without preamble.

Shentia inclined her head. "Ask, and if I can, I shall answer."

"I heard yesterday that a magic item was recently sold here in town. The source said it was some sort of armor, possibly a blend of technology and magic, maybe only magic, I can't be sure. It would've been small enough to fit in a case. Something like a briefcase was the impression I got, so it must be kind of unique."

The other woman nodded. "I've heard of such a thing,

and rumors said it had made its way to the city. Probably this is what your source is referring to. It was created a very long time ago; no one knows by whom. The pieces are a collar, two bracelets, and two ankle bands. Separately, they are useless. Once put together and invoked with the appropriate word, they create a suit of magical armor, the stored power spreading from piece to piece. It's reputed to be very powerful against both magic and mundane attacks."

Ruby breathed, "Dammit. That doesn't sound good."

"If this is in the hands of an enemy, then I very much agree with your assessment. Still, there are sure to be a few ways to overcome it. The most likely to be successful would be to overload it with concentrated damage so that a given piece fails, or to outlast it. The suit will only endure for as long as the power in the receptacles does. The final option would be to break one of the individual pieces. If one fails, they all do."

"Would it be more vulnerable to physical damage or magical damage?"

The other woman shrugged. "There's no way to be sure. Some believe a magic's opposite is more powerful against it. I think that in some cases that's true, but not always. However, I've never heard tell of what power this one uses; or, rather, I've heard multiple stories that do not match up. One says shadow, the next fire."

Ruby pictured what a full-body fire shield would look like and shuddered at the idea of having to face one. "That would be quite the impressive visual, anyway."

The Drow chuckled. "Yes, indeed it would. Imagine that in the eyes of a less sophisticated culture. That certainly argues for the possibility that the armor might have multiple magics so the wearer could use particular modes to impress different groups."

Ruby sighed. "Okay. Well, if I'm lucky, maybe I'll be wrong about having to deal with it. Perhaps some benevolent collector bought it, right?"

The dark elf lifted an eyebrow. "Almost certainly. If you believe the world tends towards goodness."

"Well, I might be in trouble then."

"Speaking of trouble, I hear news of a fracas on the surface. Some sort of warehouse. Have you heard about such a thing?"

Ruby laughed. "I'm sure your information sources are impeccable. In fact, I *do* know something about that event." She pulled the backpack off and set the bag on the case in front of her, then took out the individual pieces inside. The Drow left her chair to examine them one by one, her expertise on display as she lifted, turned, poked, and prodded.

"Impressive haul. I would not have thought you one to indulge in thievery, however."

Ruby shook her head. "Definitely not. These looked very valuable, and I didn't want them to sit in an evidence locker forever. Plenty of other, smaller stuff was around to make whatever charges they wanted stick. I hoped you might get them back to their owners, and if they can't be found, maybe you could sell them."

The Drow nodded. "I can attempt to do so. Consignment?"

She waved the idea away. "No, let's call it a credit

against future needs, in any amount you think appropriate."

The other woman laughed. "Don't you know you're not supposed to trust Drow? Everyone says so."

Ruby rolled her eyes. "If I'm ever in accordance with what everyone says, I'll know something's wrong with me. I trust everyone until they give me a reason not to."

Shentia reached under the counter and came up with a bag that she sat on the case with a *clank*. "A friend asked me to give these to you. They are healing and energy potions, contained in unbreakable metal flasks. Good for those who find themselves wading into danger on a regular basis. Or perhaps, for those who might make a habit of getting blown up in a casino."

Ruby chuckled and took them. "Thank you. Diana?"

The other woman shook her head. "No, Nylotte."

"I don't know her. Strange that she would give me a gift."

"She values Diana highly. Unless I miss my guess, you'll have the opportunity to meet Nylotte before too long. When she takes an interest in something, she's fairly tenacious about it."

"Is that common among Drow? Because it seems like it might apply to you too."

The other woman laughed. "Perhaps not among Drow, but certainly among Drow who are interested in magical objects. The trails we must follow require intense focus. So, we don't give up easily."

Ruby zipped up the backpack and shrugged it on. "Seems like good qualities to have. Thank you for your help."

Shentia nodded. "You are certainly welcome. I will try to find the owners of these pieces. Be safe."

As she opened the door, Ruby replied, "I'll do my best."

As she closed the door behind her, she was startled as another voice said, "Try your best to what?"

She turned with a growl to see her sister leaning against the building with her arms crossed. "None of your business."

"What are you up to?"

"Also none of your business, but I can see you'll keep stalking me until I tell you. I'm gathering information for the police so I can share it with Sheriff Alejo. Someone has to do something, and I know people who can find information and need someone to pass it on. I'll also share it with you when I've got it together, as I promised."

A smug look appeared on Morrigan's face. "That explains why you went in there with a full backpack and came out with an empty one, how?"

"Again, none of your business."

Her sister took a step forward, and her expression and tone became almost pleading. "Whatever you're doing, I can help. Let me."

Ruby scowled and turned away, calling back, "No, you can't. Now go home."

Right at the edge of her hearing, she heard her sister's muttered, "We'll see about that."

***

After returning home to pick up Idryll, she portaled to the garage and headed back into her house. *One of these days,*

I'm gonna confess what I am to my roommates so I can quit having to use the garage and portal in and out of the house. This is ridiculous. Still, part of her understood that her parents wouldn't bother to keep it secret without reason, and given the need to keep other secrets in her life now, maintaining this one wasn't nearly as annoying as it had been. She found Demetrius playing video games with Shiannor and watched for a while. When he lost a round of Mario Kart, she tapped him on the shoulder. He looked up. "Cutting in?"

She laughed. "No, but I hoped to talk with you. In private."

Shiannor lifted an eyebrow and made a lascivious *woo* sound, and she gave him a mock scowl. "In your dreams, pointy."

"That's entirely racist, you round-eared barbarian," he replied neutrally. It was a thing they did, and neither took offense.

Demetrius's room was closer, and he flopped down on his bed as she sat backward on his task chair. He asked, "Okay, what can I do for you?"

For an entirely unexpected moment, she *really* wanted to join him on the bed and see where that might lead. Instead, she closed her eyes and forced her attention back to where it belonged. "I have to ask you for a favor, a big one. You'll get a retainer paid by Spirits, but that will take a week or two to arrange."

"I'm listening." He propped himself up on his elbows to see her better.

"I need to know what's going on in this town. Whenever something bad is happening, I want to hear about it right away. Like an early warning system. You're usually on your computer, and I know you can hack into anything you want to, so I figure you're the right person to ask."

"Why?" The fact that he didn't protest his inability to do it gave her hope.

"It's for the good of the city. We have to stop these people, and if you tell me, then I can tell others. Because of who my family is, they might listen."

"Why are *you* getting involved? How does this affect you?"

She squeezed the back of the chair with her fingers. "It's not about me. Someone has to do this, and I can. I have advantages that others don't. That puts me in a good position."

He thought about it for a second, then nodded. "Okay. I'll help, and I'll ask the others what they've seen and heard. But know this. I'm not going to follow orders blindly. If I think something's weird, I'll do what I feel like I need to do, including calling the police, the sheriff, the FBI, whatever. I won't out you or anything, but I also won't keep secrets that could lead to people getting hurt."

Ruby nodded. "I can't ask for more than that." She reached into her thigh pocket and pulled out an earpiece. "This is an encrypted communicator to allow us to stay in touch. It's comfortable enough to wear most of the time if you want, but we can use phones for most of our connections. It's just that if I'm going to investigate something you find, or whatever, it would be nice to be able to communicate with you." She tossed it across the room, and he caught it easily.

"Did you make this?"

She nodded. "I helped. Margrave did most of the work."

Demetrius frowned. "Ruby, are you sure you know what you're doing?"

She rose out of the chair and slapped the back of it with a palm. "One hundred percent. Absolutely."

He laughed. "Sounds like a lie."

She shrugged, grinned, and headed for the door. "Thanks, Demetrius. I knew I could count on you." *All the support pieces are in place. Now it's on me not to screw it up.*

CHAPTER TWENTY-TWO

Goryo lay on the bed in his rented house, staying as motionless as possible so the custom blend of healing medicines he'd taken could do their work. It wasn't as good as the potions the magicals had, but it would still get him on his feet faster than without it. His eyes were closed, and his earpiece fed sound from the listening devices he'd left behind at the security company. He usually downloaded the information and listened at his leisure, but he was bored, so he was eavesdropping in real-time.

When the two owners' voices had come through the receiver in the garage, he'd climbed up out of a half-sleep to listen more intently. They entered the car they regularly used together, based on the fact that he heard them conversing on that pickup fairly often. The human asked, "So, everything's good for tonight?"

The dwarf replied, "Definitely. We have the best of the best ready to go."

"Any change in the objectives?"

A short laugh. "I'm going to give them free rein to cause

as much havoc as possible. Avoiding civilian casualties where possible, of course. We'll beat on the security personnel and the people who work there if they do anything other than run away, though. Plus, we'll do everything we can to damage the casino enough that it's forced to close. If the owners are there, we'll take them down."

The other man muttered something inaudible, then continued, "If only we could've nabbed the kid on our first attempt, we'd be moving onto another place already." The worry in his voice was unmistakable.

His partner spoke in a low, calm tone, clearly attempting to soothe his companion. "Don't worry about it. My people will get us back on track tonight. Then the boss can point us at our next target. We're already thinning the competition, everything's moving in the right direction, and it all looks good going forward. Try not to freak out too much."

The human laughed. "Screw you."

"There's the Jared we all know and love." Their conversation turned to unimportant things, and Goryo flicked off the receiver. *So, they're going after the Atlantean casino. Makes sense. That's something I can use to my benefit.*

He forced himself up out of bed with a groan and headed for the laptop computer on the desk in the house's small office. A few keystrokes called up the Kraken's blueprints, provided by the best infomancer he knew, and he examined them carefully. *Okay, when things start to happen downstairs, it will freak out the owners and their kid. They'll retreat to the secure floor in the casino and hold there to see what happens, most likely. If I can move into position, I can hit them when they get there, or at least kidnap the child. I need to know more than I do now.*

He clicked the icon to launch a secure communication program his magical computer genius had provided and typed.

Free for twelve?

A message came back almost instantly.

Can be.

Standard rates?

Sure.

Excellent. Here's what I need you to do.

He gave the infomancer several things to research, a series of actions to take immediately, and others to do when the action kicked off. He promised to send a signal to trigger the latter when he saw the security company moving. Closing the app deleted the information and over-wrote the memory that had contained it.

He showered quickly and headed for the walk-in closet that held his gear. He slipped on the same outfit he'd worn before, with an undamaged set of fitted body armor under-neath. Only three of the protective sheaths had come with him to Ely, and he couldn't reuse them until his armorer had replaced whatever required replacing. He strapped his pistols into place and slid a dart gun with custom ammuni-tion into the holster at the small of his back.

Next up was the harness for his sword, which he shrugged on and adjusted to ensure it was positioned properly for an over-the-shoulder draw. Any hesitation could be fatal when matters were up-close like they would be if he had to turn to the blade. Then he opened the case that contained his secret weapon. He slipped on the bracelets and ankle cuffs, then snapped the collar closed around his neck. He covered it all with a dark jacket that zipped up past the collar and had a slit that allowed the hilt of the sword to stick out. Pockets held extra magazines for his pistols and several other potentially useful tools. Fully equipped, he headed to the garage to start his drive to the casino.

Grentham hopped out of the car and walked toward the door to the storage space he'd rented, as always through a deniable third party. The SUV peeled out behind him, his partner wanting to make sure he was as far from the action as it was possible to be. *As usual.* Grentham shook his head. *He'd say it's good business. I think if it looks like cowardice and acts like cowardice, it's probably cowardice. But what the hell do I know? I'm not going in tonight either.*

Waiting inside the large building were his two bodyguards and the team he'd send in to take on the Atlanteans that night. Unlike the last action, this crew included magicals and humans to overwhelm the casino security, both with numbers and power. He didn't doubt there would be some magicals among their guards, but that's what overwhelming force was designed for, taking on more powerful enemies.

He made a gesture so they would stay seated and climbed up on an ammunition crate to ensure they could all see him. "Okay, people. Here's the deal. You're going to go into the Kraken and create as much trouble as possible. Break things, take out the guards, steal money from the casino if you can, but be sure you make a total mess of the place. I want them to have no option but to close for some *serious* renovation, get me?"

Nods and smiles traveled around the room, and one bold soul confirmed, "We get you."

Grentham nodded. "Good. Primary objective is what I said. Wreck the casino and take out its security. While most of you are causing chaos on the first floor, a team will go up into the administrative offices to secure whatever confidential materials happen to be available. If we can find the owners, they become the main priority for that group. I can't imagine they'll stay; odds are they'll portal out at any sign of danger. If you get a sense that they're present, eliminating them becomes the most important thing." His team's expressions showed they wouldn't have any problem pulling the trigger on the casino owners, which meant he'd chosen his people wisely.

"Finally, if you get any suggestion of significant force coming against you, whether it's additional guards, police, whatever, drop smoke grenades and get the hell out. Hit, fade, and fight another day. Cars will be waiting a block away, right where we planned. Do as much damage as you can without getting dead. Any questions?"

None came. "Okay. Vans are outside. Get a move on."

Ruby's burner phone rang, and she laughed as she answered. "Demetrius, you're right down the hall."

His tone drove her mirth away. "There's a hack underway on all the casinos and the Ely PD. It has a signature I recognize from an infomancer who goes by the handle Scimitar. She's one of the best and has been linked to criminal enterprises around the world. She's like a hero among hackers. I can't imagine why she'd be messing around here."

Ruby frowned. "Unless it's part of something bigger, you mean. I get it. I'll have the comm turned on from here on out, and I'll head out to the Strip and see what I can see."

"Be careful." He clicked off before she could reply.

She said, "All right, kitty cat, let's get a move on." They dressed quickly, identically to their last outing. Ruby had found a slightly better way to hold the throwing knives, and they now rested in tiny sheaths on her belt, still loose enough to grab and throw in a single action. Her partner must've felt the same seriousness she did because Idryll offered no witty banter and made no effort to avoid wearing the disguise.

Ruby nodded in approval when they were both geared up. "Well, you wanted an interesting life, right? Let's go find one." She summoned a portal, and they stepped through to an alley at one end of the Strip.

CHAPTER TWENTY-THREE

Ruby tapped the comm device in her ear through her mask. "Glam?"

The tech's voice came back an instant later. "Ruby, what do you need?"

"There's action going down, right now. Cyber attack that seems unlikely to be the start and end of something. Can you help me out?"

Deacon's voice came across the channel. "Of course we can. What do you need?"

"The infomancer is going after all the casinos on the Strip and the PD as well, according to my local computer wizard. Doesn't make sense, unless—

"Unless it's a smokescreen for a concentrated attack on one of them," Glam interrupted. "I get you. Traffic cameras?"

Deacon answered, "Traffic cameras."

Ruby said to Idryll, "They're helping us. Breaking into the traffic cameras, I guess to see if they can spot anything weird."

The tiger woman nodded. "Excellent. Perhaps I should have an earpiece, too."

"If there's anyone I could admit your existence to, I would think it would be safe to do it with them. I'm not sure the magic of the *venamisha* would agree, though."

Her partner shrugged. "You could try."

Ruby grinned. "I could try."

Glam's voice broke in. "Deacon's spotted three vans moving in a way that looks coordinated. They're headed toward the other end of the Strip and are currently at about the midpoint."

"Okay, hang on. We'll get closer." Ruby opened a portal, and she and Idryll skipped through to a spot between The Hunt and the Kraken.

Glam reported, "Vans drove up the sidewalk to the Kraken and stopped outside the casino doors. People with guns are piling out."

"Got it." She assumed the techs had a drone in action somewhere to have that information. Ruby threw a veil around herself and Idryll, and they headed off at a run. "Can you contact the Ely PD?"

Glam answered, "Negative. Communication is down."

Ruby replied, "Hang on a sec." They were close enough to see the vans, which looked utterly normal aside from their location and the wide-open doors. She activated her other comm to Demetrius. "It's going down at the Kraken. Can you get hold of the police or the sheriff?"

After a pause, he replied, "No. They're blocked. Nothing's getting in or out. Probably they'll notice before too long and be on the move."

"Dammit. Okay. Let me know if anything changes." She

clicked back over to the other comm unit. "My guy can't get to them either."

Glam offered, "We can notify the PDA, but their response time will suck, and we've already discussed they're going to bring suspicion of everyone and everything along with them."

Ruby considered that for a second, but it really wasn't a question. "If they can help, send them." She'd deal with whatever fallout she had to after they ended the threat.

Glam replied, "Affirmative," as Ruby and Idryll dashed through the doors into the casino.

Appropriate to its name, the Kraken was oceanic from start to finish. The lighting moved to give the impression of being underwater, projections traveled on the walls as if they were giant monsters swimming by, and everything reinforced the notion that you were below the waves, walking on the bottom of the ocean. However, the gunfire and explosions coming from all around and the constant chill rain of the sprinkler system wrecked the atmosphere. Ruby growled, "I have no idea how many of them there are."

Idryll replied, "Me either. Let's make sure that number gets smaller."

"Excellent plan. Meet at the escalators?"

The other woman grinned. "Perfect."

Idryll charged to the left, heading directly for the nearest invader. It was easy to identify them since they all wore at least a piece or two of military gear that differed from the uniforms required of the casino security personnel. The cacophony was unlike anything she'd ever experienced since her rivals and prey on Oriceran tended to be exclusively non-technological. Still, television had shown her these things, so it wasn't completely unfamiliar. Her target never saw her coming, and she smashed into him with a full-body leap, her forearms crashing into his ear under his helmet. His weapon flew into the air, and he made a speedy trip that ended with his back slamming into the floor. She landed on him and punched his face, both blows making sure he wouldn't get up anytime soon, then looked for the next.

He saw her at the same time she spotted him. Bullets sped toward her, but she skittered to the side, changing her direct approach to a zigzag, and moved too quickly for him to track her with his rifle. He panicked and tried to backpedal at the last moment, which only worked to her advantage. A push at his throat and an ankle kick knocked him to the floor, then she leapt and dropped to both knees on his chest. A cracking sound came from beneath the armor he wore, and he expelled blood in a cough. She peered down at him and shook her head sadly. "I might've broken this one. Pity. You're all so fragile."

Her instincts warned her of trouble, and she dove off to the side and rolled away in time to avoid being caught by the grenade she'd sensed coming through the air. It blew up the man she'd injured, as well as the gaming tables around him. Fortunately, most of the casino workers had fled, and only guards remained behind to mix it up with the attackers.

Idryll rose to her feet and turned a slow circle to find

that three hard-faced men were pointing rifles at her. She bared her teeth in a fierce grin, predator to prey. "Well, this should be fun."

Ruby moved to her right, summoning her full-body force shield as well as a buckler on her arm. It was enough of a drain that she could sense it pulling at her pool of power, but it wouldn't stop her from fighting with weapons or attacking magically if necessary. Plus, she had two healing potions and two energy potions in her thigh pockets, meaning she could afford to be a little less frugal with her power than usual. *If I ever needed a solid defense, it's in this mess.*

It was hard to isolate who might be a danger, given the sheer number of the attackers. She estimated a couple of dozen, at least, but the situation was so fluid she couldn't be sure. The thought crossed her mind that it would be quite convenient to be able to pick off some of them from a distance, but she wasn't adequate with a pistol and wouldn't tie up both hands with a bow. *Plus, there's something satisfying about being up close.* She drew her sword with her right hand and layered force magic over the blade, not willing to deliver instantly fatal wounds if she could avoid doing so. Everyone would benefit if the attackers survived to be grilled for information. While those who'd already fallen in the casino perhaps deserved eye-for-an-eye justice, she needed to focus on the bigger picture, what was best for the city.

The first enemy she found was unaware of her presence

as he traded shots with guards on the second floor, at the top of the long escalator designed to look like a coral reef that served as the room's centerpiece. He wore a helmet that protected the back of his head, so instead of the elbow she might've used against a defenseless foe, she snapped her sword out in a horizontal strike and bashed him at temple height. He stumbled forward and didn't move after he hit the floor.

The action caused another nearby attacker to notice her, and in an instant, rifle bullets were on the way. *Damn. These people are as good as anyone I've faced on this planet.* She interposed her shield to catch them and charged in that direction. Before she got there, a second bad guy noticed her and fired from a different angle. Ruby threw herself across a poker table, landing hard on the far side and dropping her sword. She popped up and threw a force blast at the nearest, catching him in the chest and sending him flying backward through the air. The second one dove for cover behind a pillar, evading the magical attack she sent in his direction and leaned out to fire a moment later.

She caught his rounds on her shield, then knelt to retrieve her sword, and sheathed it. After casting a veil, she crept out from behind the table, moving in a circular path toward the back of the pillar. He never heard her coming, and she kicked out his legs from beneath him and did a small hop to land on his shoulder blades, her heels slamming into them with a pair of resounding *cracks*. She kicked his weapon away and moved ahead, looking for the next target.

The veil had cost her some energy, but she still had enough for a while at least. More practice with magic would build her reserve, Keshalla had said, and she'd made it part of her daily routine. Still, she never had enough to do all that she thought she should be able to do, and the scientist portion of her mind wondered if, as her magic increased in power, it also became proportionately more costly. In any case, she felt safe being visible as long as she didn't wind up the focus of multiple enemies at once.

Despite her efforts to be careful and look out for any kind of potential trouble, it was a total surprise when the dark elf stepped out of nowhere and blasted her with a double dose of lightning.

CHAPTER TWENTY-FOUR

Ruby clashed her bracelets together, summoning a barrier of force that materialized as a dome around her, cutting off the oncoming magic. It took several seconds for the jitters of that lightning blast slamming her shield to subside, after which she drew her sword and readied herself for battle with the elf. She poured more energy into the buckler on her left arm, increasing its size until it was almost her full height.

The barrier fell, and she charged her foe. He cast magical attacks with both hands, seemingly unconcerned with defense, and maneuvered to the side to avoid her rush. She caught blasts of shadow and fire on her shield, wincing as the power fed back into her. Still, it was only a tiny fraction of what it would be without that protection. She got close enough to whip her sword around in a strike at his chest, and he blocked it with a hastily summoned shadow shield in his left hand as a shadow blade extended from his right.

Before she could recover for a second stroke, he was on

her, his blade lashing out in a series of fast attacks. *Should've stuck with the casting, buddy.* Part of her training with Keshalla included a variety of fighting styles to defend against, and she recognized what the Drow was using. It relied on speed, trying to overwhelm the opponent to the degree that they got in the way of their reflexes. Ruby used the appropriate defense, letting her mind go soft and trusting that her body would do what she needed without too much overt control.

Her sword licked out to deflect the first blow of the next flurry and batted his weapon upward, wrecking whatever pattern he'd planned. She slashed hers inward but met his shield. He snapped out a kick, and she skipped backward, then hacked her blade down at the extended leg. He yanked it back and launched himself at her, shield held in front of him like a battering ram. She caught it on hers, meeting his force with hers and trusting in her strength to counteract his slight build. She held, breaking his momentum.

He spun to disconnect from her shield and whipped his sword around. She ducked under the swipe and took a force blast as he abandoned melee attacks and let his defensive magic fade. The shield that lay an inch away from her skin caught the magic and spread the power equally across her body. With a grunt, she slashed low at his legs. The only evasive option he had was to leap, and he took it, rendering him vulnerable for a moment as he sent another blast of magic in her direction.

She took advantage of his defenselessness, abandoning the shield in her left hand and smashing him with a beam of force. He brought up a force disc to protect his head, figuring that's where the attack would be coming, so her bolt smashed unhindered into his undefended groin. He fell with a hard *thump* and curled up in pain. She took a step toward him to make sure he was unconscious but caught gunfire out of the corner of her eye and crouched behind her shield as a pair of humans on the escalator attacked her.

Idryll crouched suddenly, and the initial flurry of shots went over her head. The trio had positioned themselves so they didn't catch each other in a crossfire, a situation she hoped to change quickly. She leapt forward, staying low, and smashed into the knees of the nearest with her full momentum behind her. The joints snapped, and the man went up over her back and down to the floor as she plowed through him without halting.

She cut immediately to the right, assuming the others would be drawing a bead, and took an angle on one of the remaining two that put him between her and the third. Bullets flew, a couple of them close enough to pluck at her clothes as she advanced. The nearer man dropped his rifle and went for knives, a pair of wicked-looking serrated blades that ended in a sharp point appearing in his fists.

Idryll halted her rush to avoid impaling herself, and he flicked the weapons out at her in a series of cuts at her face and hands. He was good, and despite her speed advantage, she didn't have all that much experience fighting men with knives. She did know claws though and knew their weaknesses quite well. She batted attacks aside and bided her time, moving on a path opposite the third, who was trying to find an angle that would get her current opponent out of the way. Finally, her foe made a mistake, only a small one, extending his arm a little too far to reach her.

She popped out her claws and slashed the underside of his arm, tearing the muscle and forcing him to drop the blade. He recoiled in shock, and she repeated the process on the other arm, slicing through the flesh underneath. Then she stepped forward and delivered a front kick to his torso, sending him flying into the one behind him. They both smashed to the floor, and before the unwounded one could react, she jumped on him and stabbed her claws deep into his shoulders, ensuring he wouldn't use his arms anytime soon.

The screams of pain almost caused her to miss Ruby's shout. "Kitty cat, upstairs." She turned and saw that Ruby held up a shield to block attacks from people on the escalator. With a growl, she charged for the moving staircase in the middle of the room.

***

Ruby considered taking out the pair on the moving staircase with force bolts, but she had business on the second floor anyway, so it was time to move. Running up the escalator was a nonstarter since she'd be a target on the approach. Instead, she blasted the floor beneath her with force magic, sending her hurtling toward her foes. She arced over the men and landed on the far side, then placed a hand on the metal between the sides and vaulted it, snapping a foot into the face of the nearest. He crumpled and rolled down the stairs.

The other one produced a knife from nowhere, so she coated her left arm with an additional force magic layer and used it as a blocker. He kept her at a distance with his thrusts, making her focus on defense while they climbed higher. She threw a punch now and again that he blocked with elbows, but the available space on the escalator didn't allow for much more. Retreating wasn't an option for fear of a misstep that would send her plunging down the staircase, and every time she tried to punch, he moved the knife in the way to block. She readied a force bolt, but her partner's move rendered it unnecessary.

Idryll, moving as fast as she'd ever seen her run, dashed up the down stairs. She leapt over the separator and smashed an elbow into the man's head, and he tipped over the side and fell to the floor below.

Ruby commented, "Subtle."

The tiger woman laughed. "I didn't rip out his heart or bite off his arm. You should count that as a gift to protect your delicate sensibilities."

Ruby gestured upward. "Those folks up there might need some of the same treatment." She stepped forward, slipping past her partner and raising a force shield to catch the inbound gunfire. She curved the barrier as they went, making sure she covered their flanks. "I'll go left."

"You're remarkably inconsistent. You know that?"

She barked a laugh. "Everyone's a critic. Shut it. I think there's a bunch of these guys up here, so be careful." They separated at the top, Ruby charging the ones to the left, who had dropped their rifles in favor of pistols and spread apart. Gunfire hit her shield as she approached, biting like bee stings and pulling at her magical reserves, but she continued. She snapped a kick out at the first one, who seemed utterly amazed that his bullets weren't reaching her, and he went down in a lump.

Ruby turned to the other, who had yanked out a baton that sparked at the end. "Seriously?" She let her shield fall and bathed him with lightning, and he dropped twitching to the floor. "Idiots."

A deep voice sounded from nearby. "They *are* idiots, you're right. I imagine you'll find me a greater challenge." She turned to see a dwarf with scars on his face and hands, hefting a battle ax.

She shook her head. "I don't think so, short stuff."

She repeated the lightning attack, and he raised the ax, which glowed as it sucked in her magic and nullified it. His grin widened. "Oh, you're gonna pay for that comment."

Idryll took care of the first two enemies with no problem, humans both, who wound up flying over the railing toward the bottom floor. The appearance of a wizard was unexpected, and she only realized he was there when a bolt of shadow slammed into her side and knocked her sprawling. Fortunately, she was low enough to fetch up against the railing before she followed the others over the edge. She scrambled to get out of the way and ducked behind tables and chairs to evade further attacks. He seemed to be mixing force and shadow, based on the number of things that went flying past her as she ran.

He had a better position, a clear, cover-free area where he could attack her if she moved toward him. It was a frustrating situation, made more so because she was in her humanoid form. Her tiger form was faster, and she would feel far more comfortable about her ability to reach him before getting struck were she in it. Still, this form had hands, which could be useful. She picked up a table and hurled it at the wizard. He batted it aside with a look of condescension, but a chair was already flying at him. Idryll advanced behind her improvised missiles, throwing one after the next, cutting the distance between them with each projectile.

When she was halfway there, he realized he was in trouble and threw up a wall of flame. Unfortunately for him, the barrier blocked vision in both directions, and he'd only made it about eight feet high. Idryll dashed forward, jumped up on a table that looked solid enough to handle her weight, and vaulted in a somersault over the top. The wizard didn't realize she was there until she landed beside him and snapped out a quick jab to the side of his head. He staggered sideways, and she stepped outward and pivoted her hips to deliver a right cross to his temple. He went down, completely limp before his body slammed to the ground. Idryll grabbed his wand and regarded it for a second before snapping it in two, then turned to look for Ruby.

CHAPTER TWENTY-FIVE

Ruby threw a couple more spells at the dwarf, but that ax kept interposing itself and eating the magic. Fire, lightning, no effect. She drew her dagger in her left hand and spun the sword in her right, then stepped forward to meet him in the open space that separated them. "I have other things to do rather than kill you. You could go now and avoid dying."

He spun the ax in both hands, and the heavy weapon moved so rapidly, it looked like nothing more than a toy. She positioned herself appropriately; her body turned perpendicular to him to provide the smallest possible target. She wanted to look for Idryll, to know whether she was okay or not, but couldn't afford the distraction. He lunged forward with a downward chop, an inelegant move that was nonetheless so fast it almost snuck through. She stepped her back foot out wide and swung the dagger across to slap against the blade and push it out of line. She flicked it to cast a quick force bolt at him that he weathered with a grunt. He said, "Tricky. Should've kept that one in reserve, little cat."

"Leopard," she growled and stabbed in with her sword. He brought the shaft of the ax over to block. She went with that momentum, spinning around to slam a backhand at his head. He caught it before it struck and yanked her off balance. She intentionally kept going in the direction he'd moved her, diving forward and bumping into a table at the end. She hopped up in time to be hit with a shadow bolt coming from the top of his ax. It fed back through her shield and she gave a small moan of pain and forced words between her gritted teeth. "You have some tricks yourself, shorty."

He laughed and charged, spitting magic from his free hand while chambering an attack with the ax. She set herself, waited for the right moment, and snapped out a beam of force at his feet. He tripped, and the weapon flew at her head. She batted it aside with her sword and moved forward, only for the thing to come flying back to his hand a moment later. She slid to a stop, panting. "Nice trick. Maybe you could teach me."

He shrugged. "Join our side, help us do our job, we can talk."

"No chance."

"Too bad." He raised his voice and shouted, "Boys?"

Two more dwarves with similar axes stepped out from behind some sort of magical concealment, one each off to the left and right of her current foe. She grimaced and muttered, "That's going to be a problem."

Idryll spotted her partner across the floor facing off against a dwarf but was unable to intervene. A giant Kilomea stood in her path, having thumped his way up the escalator a moment before. He'd seen her immediately upon gaining the second floor and had headed toward her in a lumbering jog. He was easily eight feet tall, muscles on top of muscles, and moved with far too much grace for someone that size. She knew that was part of their magic, part of what made them incredibly deadly. He held no weapon, but it didn't make him any less dangerous. Taking a punch from those fists, or worse, getting caught by those hands would be quickly fatal.

She advanced toward him slowly, all her senses sharp, ready for whatever he might do. He seemed content to meet her in the middle, in a small area free of obstacles. Her palms ached with the desire to snap out her claws, but since he wouldn't be impressed, doing so before she needed to use them made no sense. The boots she wore interfered with her balance a little, and she wished she could be without them, but time didn't permit that, either. When they reached a distance slightly outside of combat range, they began to circle, as if by unspoken agreement. The look of anticipation on his face was almost pleasurable, and it drove a spike of irritation through her. *Oh, you think it's going to be that easy, do you? You need to learn a lesson about the relationship between size and prowess.* She said, "One chance. Go now and live. Fight me, and you won't survive."

He laughed deep and low, lifted a hand, and beckoned her forward. She accepted the invitation and charged. He spread his feet as she advanced, appearing as if his goal was to grab her when she tried to make her attack. She feinted low, then went to one side, trailing an arm behind to rake her claws against the leather trousers that covered his thigh. They skittered across the tough surface and cut parallel furrows into it but failed to penetrate. She ducked his casual swing easily and backed up, staring down at her hand. Her claws were fine, which meant he was probably wearing some sort of highly reinforced or magical armor. *Well, that'll make things more difficult.*

He moved with a quickness she wouldn't have expected as he crossed the distance between them and snapped out a kick. She leapt to the side to avoid it and barely evaded his grasping fingers by twisting further to the side. The move carried her into a table, and it fell backward as she regained her balance. He closed while she recovered and launched a flurry of punches that she escaped with a combination of dodges and redirections. The power of his blows was immense, and she couldn't go strength versus strength with him in this form. She raked her claws across the muscles in his arms when she could, but the armor continued to protect him.

He blasted out a heavy punch with his right hand, and she barely dodged it in time. The distraction allowed him to catch her with the back of his left, and she went flying to crash into a table and chairs, rolling over them and landing hard on the floor. She pushed herself unsteadily to her feet, her head ringing, and readied herself for his next attack.

Ruby backpedaled slowly, and the dwarves moved to keep the distance between them consistent. She snapped a force bolt at the one on the far left with her dagger, but he blocked it with a shield on his left arm. *Well, at least maybe not* all *their weapons absorb magic, so that's something.* She'd faced multiple opponents armed with physical weapons before, but a trio of casters provided a unique challenge that threw her mind into a series of whirls and spins. She asked, "I don't suppose we could postpone this so I can follow your friends up to the third level, could we?" She'd seen the invaders moving through the door to the higher level and figured they were after the owners again, assuming they were present at the casino.

The trio shook their heads, and the first one she'd fought said, "See, you should've joined up when you had the chance."

Ruby set her stance and waited for one of them to make a move. When the attack arrived, it was all three at once. The one on the left cast a shadow bolt she caught with her shield. Lightning crashed in from the far right, and it ate away at the force barrier on her body, draining her. The third rushed in with his ax, ready to cleave her in two. With no other good option, she smashed her bracelets together again, summoning the dome of force and locking them outside. She scrabbled at her thigh and found an energy potion, flipped open the lid, and drank it. The pleasurable surge of the magic coursing through her almost made her pant with joy. She readied herself, still not sure how she would take on the trio, but as ready as she could be. Then the shield fell, and the dwarves came in again.

She circled to her left, hoping to at least put one of them at a bad angle, and used the shield on that arm to catch more magical attacks from the one on that side. The dwarf in the middle seemed to think he needed to handle her in a more personal fashion and stalked toward her with his ax at the ready. She faced the choice of shifting the shield in his direction and hoping the one that covered her body would be sufficient to handle what the left-side enemy was throwing at her when an arrow streaked in and smashed into the floor beside the caster.

A force burst exploded from the tip and sent him flying. Ruby didn't wait to figure out what was going on but charged at the dwarf in the middle. A wide smile appeared on his face as he slashed his ax down in a diagonal strike. She used a force blast to lift herself up and over him, landing in front of the one whose angle had been blocked. She stabbed with her sword, no longer covered with a safety shield, and pierced his leg and arm with two quick thrusts, forcing him to drop his ax. She spun and delivered a sidekick to his chest, and he flew over the railing and dropped.

Looking for her benefactor, she spotted a hooded form crouched atop one of the lights that hung from the ceiling, already nocking another arrow aimed at a different part of the upper floor, and said a quiet word of thanks. Ruby turned back to the dwarf and smiled. "Okay, now, where were we?"

CHAPTER TWENTY-SIX

Idryll staggered to her feet and dodged out of the way as the mammoth Kilomea smashed through the tables and chairs toward her. Her leg hurt enough to make her limp, and fury clouded her mind, turning her vision red. She snarled at her enemy, and his laughter doubled her anger. He taunted, "Come here, pretty little kitty. I will taste the marrow in your bones."

She charged with a snarl, to all outward appearances lost in rage. However, Idryll was never that far out of control. He spread his hands wide to catch her, and she feigned a jump, then slid and delivered a kick to his knee. It buckled, dropping him, and she barely got out from underneath in time. She bounced up while turning and punched her claws at his neck, but he rolled forward with a sound like a tree falling and came up to his feet, spinning a back fist in her direction. Ducking under it, she stabbed upward only to find her wrist locked in his grip. A slash at the tendons in his wrist again failed to penetrate the tough hide of the armor he wore. She went for his bare hand instead, scraping bloody furrows in it, then slashed at the other one as his fingers loosened in reflex to the pain.

A new enemy appeared in the corner of her eye as she danced backward. She spun with a hiss toward the man who pointed a rifle at her, but she had no chance of reaching him before he pulled the trigger. An arrow struck him out of nowhere, and a blast of force magic hurled him into the wall, the loud *crack* signaling breaking bones. She didn't question the lucky turn of events, only turned and charged at the Kilomea. It seemed as if he hadn't noticed someone else had joined the fight, so when the archer's next arrow hit him in the back and propelled him forward, he wasn't ready for it. Idryll was.

She jumped toward her foe and wrapped her arm around his neck, curling her body over to sit on his shoulders. Jamming her claws into the gap between his armor and the flesh of his chest, she sank them deep into his muscles. She curled them, ripped them out in a spray of blood, and hopped off as he fell. It was a grievous wound although possibly not fatal if he kept enough pressure on it. She turned as the archer landed beside her. It was a Mist Elf, and one she recognized—Ruby's sister. Her outfit was all about anonymity, a voluminous black hooded cloak that disguised her body and a matching balaclava covering her face. The woman nodded at her, then moved in her sibling's direction.

Now that the odds were one-on-one again, Ruby craved the pleasure of bringing down this opponent. Even if she hadn't wanted that closure so badly, she couldn't safely leave him at her back, so her desire and needs were in alignment. She waded in and traded blows and blocks, her sword meeting the ax again and again, chimes ringing out at each intersection. She spotted motion from the corner of her eye but couldn't spare the attention to see if it was an ally or an enemy. *I need to end this fight and fast.*

She banished the force buckler on her left arm and reached down to her belt, releasing one of the containers that held the special items Margrave had given her. Stepping backward, she slammed it on the floor between them, and the smoke and glitter rose in a sudden rush to completely occlude them from one another. She called up her veil and circled away and was nowhere in sight when the distraction dissipated. She charged from behind and slashed at his legs, cutting bloody lines through the back of each of his thighs. He shouted in pain and tried to spin and swing his ax but fell to the floor partway through the motion. She grabbed his weapon and announced, "I'm taking this with me. Always happy to go for round two if you want it back."

She turned with her sword defensively raised as people neared, then her mouth opened in shock at the sight of the woman next to Idryll. Even with the balaclava covering most of her face, her sister's eyes were unmistakable. She stammered, "Who are you? What are you doing here?"

"Ruby, please. Don't be an idiot."

She sighed. "Fine, but what are you doing here?"

"Saving your ass, pretty much."

"I don't suppose it's worth telling you to go home?" Her

sister shook her head. "Fine, come with us. I saw a bunch of them go up to the third floor."

They dashed across to the stairwell, Ruby leading the way in complete disbelief that her sister was here. Her accuracy with the bow was no surprise; she'd seen her sister's skill with the weapon before, and her abilities equaled those of anyone she'd ever seen aside from Keshalla. How she'd wound up with magic-tipped arrows was an important conversation for another day.

She pounded up the stairwell and out into the casino's main administrative area, the refreshing fact that the sprinklers on this floor weren't active an immediate bonus. A glass-walled office sat in the corner, with the Atlantean casino owners huddled in the back of it. All three of them had their hands out, working together to maintain a defensive shield against the attacks the magicals and humans arranged around them in a semi-circle poured into it. Morrigan asked, "Why haven't they portaled?"

Ruby shook her head, wondering the same thing. "Probably thought they'd be fine, then got caught with a rush and feel unsafe letting down the barrier to cast the portal. Stupid, arrogant, overconfident."

Idryll chuckled. "Sounds like someone in our group as well."

"Don't talk about my sister that way." She knew that Morrigan was sticking her tongue out at her even though she couldn't see it. "Okay, here's what we're going to do. I'll take the ones on the left, and you take the one on the right. The masked moron provides backup. All we need to do is knock them off balance long enough for the Atlanteans to portal out of here."

Morrigan said, "I've got this." She reached over her shoulder to draw an arrow by touch and came out with one with a bright red tip. Ruby groaned, "Oh, hell no," before her sister loosed the missile. It shattered the glass wall, landed at the attackers' feet, and detonated, sending a wash of fire through the room.

The Chentashes took advantage of the distraction as Ruby had predicted they would, one of them maintaining a thinner barrier while another created a portal. An instant later they were gone, and the rift collapsed. The sprinkler system activated, drenching them all again, and Ruby shook her head. "Don't suppose you have sleep gas or something in there?"

Her sister shook her head. "Nope. I could hit them with more force, though."

"Let's retreat and find a better plan." It turned out they didn't need to, as the attackers in that room picked themselves up, broke the windows, and jumped, the magicals holding onto the humans to carry them to safety. Ruby tapped her earpiece. "Glam, the bad guys just ran away. What's the deal?"

The tech replied immediately. "PDA is in the building, and the attackers are bailing out. I have some bad news. The casino owners portaled to someplace weird. They're in a garage that's covered by the casino's security systems. Deacon says it's visible from the window of the room you're in. There's no way they're safe there if the attackers are at all competent."

Ruby ran over and looked out, remembering seeing that building on a tour or a plan of the property. Sure enough, three stories below was a big parking lot with a low structure beside it. "Idryll, Morrigan, we're not done yet." She dropped the dwarf's ax and jumped, fearing that, as Glam suggested, the attackers could turn out to be competent after all.

Goryo had been prepared to make his way through the chaos inspired by the attack on the Kraken to reach his targets, but before he committed to that action, Scimitar cracked the systems of the Atlantean casino. Included among the documents she found was the catastrophic escape plan. It apparently assumed that any threat to the casino would originate from one of the other magical groups since the contingency procedure was not to portal back to the underground city as he'd expected but instead appear in a garage on the property. *I guess they're not popular with the rest of the magicals in town, or at least they think they aren't.* It wasn't a complete shock since people in power frequently made decisions based on paranoia, but it did change his plans dramatically.

Balancing safety against opportunity, he decided to see if the attackers would be the hounds that chased the prey to him. He moved into the garage after Scimitar deactivated its alarms. The space contained several vehicles, one of which was a heavily armored truck like those used to transport money securely. He figured it, or maybe the heavier than usual SUV that sat beside it would be the targets' escape vehicle. He crouched in the shadows, pistol held loosely in his right hand and the dart gun in his left, ready for whatever came next.

The infomancer gave him a play-by-play of the events in the casino as seen through the security cameras. Her synthesized voice betrayed no particular interest. They'd never met in person, and he very much wondered what she was like. Or if she was a *she* at all since, to his knowledge, *no one* had ever met her in the flesh to confirm anything about her. When the attackers cornered the family in their office, and the Paranormal Defense Agency arrived on the scene, he began to think he would need to fade away without engaging and choose a different target.

Then two cat-people and an archer who had been fighting against the invaders all along, according to Scimitar, gave the Chentashes the opportunity they needed to get out of that trap. He tensed, and a moment later the Atlanteans emerged from a door at the back of the garage with two security people ahead of them and two behind. He waited until the first arrived at the armored truck, then calmly rose from his hiding place. Two squeezes of the trigger dropped the nearest guards, the rounds perfectly placed to avoid armor and helmets, and an equal number of pulls on the dart gun's trigger took down the two adult Atlanteans.

The kid rabbited, running for the front of the garage. His guards shouted for him to wait and tried to follow, but Goryo was faster, getting the angle he needed to put those two down as well. The door banged open, the kid ran through it, and he pounded in pursuit. The chemical in the darts was a product of government research that he'd stolen, a tranquilizer strong enough to be effective against any magical smaller than a Kilomea combined with a poison that would kill them in hours if no one applied the proper antidote. If he made it back in time to capture them rather than letting them die, that would be useful. If not, he'd still have the other one to deliver to his employer, and the contract had been clear that either dead or alive would be fine by him.

As he broke through the door, he was greeted by the unexpected sight of the costumed trio landing right in front of the fleeing boy. He lifted the pistol, sighted on the nearest, and fired.

CHAPTER TWENTY-SEVEN

Ruby's leap from the window landed her far enough in front of the running Atlantean that he could skid to a stop before smashing into her. She instinctively looked behind him for pursuit, and when the masked man with the pistol burst from the garage, she reacted instantly. The bracelets chimed as she slammed them together, using their final charge to throw a protective dome around her and her companions.

She opened a portal to the abbey and pushed the stunned Atlantean through, then grabbed her sister by the arm and yanked her toward the opening. "Take care of him." Morrigan tried to resist, but Idryll gave her a boot to the backside to force her the rest of the way across, and Ruby let the rift close. The process took all the time the shield offered, and they dashed in different directions as it dissipated.

She had no idea how this person fit into the bigger picture of what was going on in her city, but he matched what the cameras had recorded during the Deep Woods attack. She summoned a shield to intercept his bullets and tried to draw his attention toward her, counting on Idryll to sneak behind him and take him out. She threw magic at him, first a force bolt that he dodged with an impressively fast move to the side, then a cone of electricity that hit him squarely. His body glowed for a moment, and when it faded, he stood undamaged.

Dammit. The armor. That threat had faded from her mind during the battle's chaos. The throwing knives were her ace in the hole, but she'd need to be closer to strike true, either at a vulnerable spot that would take him out of the fight or at one of the pieces of the magical defense. *Collar, wrists, ankles, right, I remember.* He slithered aside from Idryll's sidekick and backed toward the garage.

She couldn't use flame because of the tiger's proximity, so she tried for shadow bolts, but the armor absorbed them as well. He dodged another attack from the tiger-woman and stared into Ruby's eyes for a second. She could almost see the wheels turning in his mind, wondering whether he should run or if he wanted to make those who had stolen his prey pay the price for doing so. She'd expected him to take the first choice, but he rushed into the garage. In her ear, Glam warned, "The Atlanteans are in there."

Ruby dashed in pursuit, and Idryll caught up to her right before they reached the door. "You distract him, and I'll get the parents to safety."

Her partner unexpectedly removed her mask, handed it over, and replied, "My pleasure." As they entered the garage, Idryll's body changed, stretching, growing, transforming into the amazing tiger form she'd worn at their first meeting. She roared a warning to her prey that death had arrived and loped ahead to find him. Ruby spotted a pair of feet sticking out from behind a large truck and headed in that direction while she shoved the mask in a pocket, confident the huge feline would capture their opponent's attention quite easily.

The joy of the hunt thrilled through Idryll. Her clothes had shredded and fallen away during the change, and now she felt like herself, all rippling muscles and primal power. The garage's scents filled her nose, acrid, cloying, and mostly foreign to her, but she recognized the smell of the man who'd been outside. She'd expected it to come with a tang of fear, and her estimation of her opponent's prowess increased when she failed to detect it.

He betrayed himself with a small noise before he pulled the trigger, and she was instantly in motion, rolling to the side out of the bullets' path in plenty of time to evade them. Her claws scraped on the concrete floor, not as strong a grip as she would've liked, but perfectly adequate to her needs. She jumped and touched down on the roof of the tallest vehicle, the armored car, and leapt at him. The man fired again, and the gun clicked instead of continuing to bark. He holstered it and drew his sword, and she landed in front of him with a growl.

Her foe wove the weapon in a slow pattern, seemingly ready for whatever she might do. His free hand dropped to his thigh and pulled out the pistol that rested there. She charged before he could bring it to bear, forcing him to focus on defense. He swiped with the sword, and she crouched with her front paws, letting it slide over and past her, then slashed out in a move that would rip his leg off and allow her to exert her will upon him before administering the deathblow.

Her claws struck his thigh and slid off, completely failing to penetrate. Worse, a painful tingle of magic spread up her arm. She retreated and skittered to the side, the gun's discharge forcing her to turn and dash behind the nearest vehicle for cover. After a few moments, her limb returned to normal, and she prowled around the back of the car looking for a new angle of attack.

Ruby moved in a straight line toward the Atlanteans and took position at their shoulders. When she heard Idryll's attack, she threw down one of Margrave's capsules to hide any possibility of their foe seeing what was on the other side of the portal, and opened the tunnel to the abbey. She wrestled the first Atlantean through, then Morrigan was there to assist with the second. "Thanks. Take care of them. If this guy beats us, he'll come for them again, I'm sure."

Her sister's eyes spoke volumes about how much she wanted to join the fight, but she only nodded. "I will."

Ruby stepped back through and closed the rift, then focused on the moment at hand. She rounded another vehicle that blocked her sightline in time to see Idryll's attack on their enemy. The way she rebounded and ran for cover made Ruby rethink the idea of a frontal attack. She reached out with a line of force to grab a tray of tools sitting on a bench nearby and hurled it at the man. He interposed his sword, twitching it to intercept each projectile as they arrived, then sheathed the weapon unexpectedly. She threw lightning at him with her left hand while her right extended another force line to lift a large tire and hurl it at his head.

His armor absorbed the electricity, and he ducked under the projectile and stepped calmly to the side to let it pass. The magazine from his pistol clattered on the floor, and another one clicked into place almost immediately after. Ruby called up her buckler and strengthened the force shield around her body, then extended her arm toward the heaviest object she could see, a large metal armor plate leaning against the wall. She threw it as he fired, lifting her buckler to intercept the bullets. The first round hit like a punch in her left shoulder, wrenching her to the side, and the next one buried itself in her right thigh. The pain was greater than anything she'd ever felt, and she screamed as she spun to the floor, all her magical protections vanishing. She breathed, "Kagji," activating her last-resort shield pendant to keep her from further damage as darkness encroached on her vision.

CHAPTER TWENTY-EIGHT

Seeing Ruby go down, smelling the blood splashing out of her suddenly frail-looking body, pushed Idryll into the place where she lost consciousness of anything but the need to take down her prey. Her magic was more than changing forms, and some powers only existed in certain bodies. This one could craft a veil to obscure the sight of her, which allowed her to hunt more effectively as long as she moved quietly to avoid detection. She summoned it and faded into invisibility.

She retracted her claws and prowled forward in a low crouch, padding softly on the concrete. One eye surveyed the surface in front of her to detect things that might cause noise and betray her, and the other remained locked on her foe. He'd fired twice more at her partner, but Idryll couldn't see the results of those shots. A heartbeat that sounded as if it was struggling to continue was the only sound from that direction.

She angled at the man as he walked toward his fallen

target with a smug expression she longed to claw from his face. She instinctively understood the emotional need to close and finish off a foe, but she wasn't about to let him have that satisfaction. When he crossed in front of a large open pit, she pounced. Her strong legs threw her body forward, and she smashed into him with all her weight behind the thrust. She didn't bother with her claws, knowing they wouldn't penetrate, merely slammed him bodily to hurl him into the pit.

Dashing to Ruby, she lay down beside her and called upon another of her tiger form's powers. She'd never attempted to use it on a non-shapeshifter and had no idea if it would work on someone outside her kind. With a heart full of hope, she extended her aura over the Mist Elf and concentrated on healing.

Ruby swam up to consciousness with two dominant feelings. The first was the agonizing pain caused by the quartet of bullets lodged inside her. The second was the psychological pain of her inner voice asking in disbelief, "Did you really think that a *different* magical shield was going to work better than the other ones?"

She growled, "Shut it," whether mentally or out loud she had no idea, and used her working arm to pull a healing potion from her thigh pouch. She drank it and screamed, her back arching with even more pain as it forced the bullets out of her body and the flesh filled in the holes they'd made. It felt like it took hours, but she knew from what Keshalla had told her that it would only have been seconds. This was by far the most grievous set of wounds she'd ever had to heal. She opened her eyes to see a giant tiger staring at her and managed a grin. "Hey. That explains the bad breath. How are you doing?"

The tiger chuffed, and her mouth did that weird stretching that happened when she talked in this form. "Knocked him into a pit. He'll be back soon."

She nodded and forced herself to stand. "Okay. The pistols have to go, first priority. Then, we drop things on him or throw things at him. Shentia said the more damage we apply, the more likely we are to overwhelm his protection. So, let's get it done."

A flicker of concern crossed the tiger's face, but she rose to her feet. "I'll follow your lead." She shimmered and vanished, leaving Ruby blinking, impressed at the power of her veil. *Good idea. Two can play at that game.* She called up hers and moved away from the place where she'd almost died.

She watched quietly from the side as the man pulled himself up over the edge of the lower section used for oil changes and other maintenance. He surveyed the surrounding area, holding his pistol pointed at the ceiling but ready to use it. She reached out with force magic and grabbed a wrench, then hurled it at him. She didn't have to calculate how to make it happen consciously. The magic took care of figuring out how the object she wanted to move would get to where she wanted it to be. It slammed into his left wrist, the kinetic energy behind it knocking the weapon flying.

Before he could go after it, she dropped her veil, snapped her body shield around her, and started hurling everything that wasn't nailed down at him. He drew the sword again, holding it in two hands and weaving it through defensive strokes to intercept all her improvised projectiles. That defense was sufficient until the moment Idryll moved in, only becoming visible as she slammed into his spine and sent him hurtling forward to smash down on his face. Ruby grabbed the huge armor plate that she'd missed with before and threw it in an arc.

It smashed down on his back as he was pushing himself up, completely covering his body. A shout of pain or anger came from underneath, followed by a loud *thump* as Idryll landed on top of the steel, smashing him down again. She stayed in that spot, her weight pinning him to the concrete, and for a moment Ruby thought they had him, that the tiger could sit on the metal and keep him in place. There would be a lot of explaining to do when the PDA arrived, but it was better than getting killed trying to take him out. *Maybe we vanish and run. Yeah, smart plan. When the agents arrive, veils, portals, gone.*

That plan fell to tattered ruin as a loud explosion sent the heavy metal plate flying in one direction, threw Idryll tumbling in another, and propelled the man in a slide across the floor in a third. All she could figure was that he'd had grenades and set them off, trusting that his armor would protect him. *Bold move.*

It's now or never, Ruby thought and reached down to snag a throwing knife. She ran forward, counting on her enemy at least being momentarily distracted, and threw the blade at his neck the moment she entered a reasonable range. It was an instinctive decision, and she had no idea if it was because that was his most vulnerable spot, given that the knives weren't all that long, or if it was because she knew that's where the collar portion of the armor was. The second was already in the air to the same target as the first struck.

She charged in after the projectiles, knowing that if the throws hadn't worked, things would likely go poorly for her. Ruby was on him in an instant, sword in her right hand and dagger in her left. A shallow cut bled lightly on the side of his neck, but nothing gave her a clue whether his shield was still active or not. She slashed down with her sword, aiming for his leg. His weapon snapped out to block it, then swiped up at her face. She blocked it with the dagger and whipped out a round-house kick to the nerves that ran along the outside of his thigh.

It connected, and his sudden look of pain revealed his shield was indeed gone. He realized it as she did, and panic flickered on his face. He tossed his sword to his left hand and drew the pistol from his right holster in a blur. Three things happened almost simultaneously. First, Ruby smashed him in the forehead with a force blast channeled through her dagger, upending him. That caused his shot to go over her head and ricochet off one of the vehicles with a metallic whine. Finally, Idryll rippled into existence behind him, and her claws slashed across both his ankles, shredding his boots and severing the Achilles tendons that lay beneath.

His skull hit the concrete hard, and he was out. Ruby panted, adrenaline making her tremble, and sheathed her sword on the second try. Glam's voice came over her earpiece. "Nice fight. I have a recording from a drone in there if you want to watch it later. Right now, the PDA is headed your way, and you should get the hell out."

Ruby replied, "Thanks. Come on, kitty cat, help me gather up some of his stuff, and let's vacate the premises." By the time the agents burst into the garage with guns drawn, the only people left inside were four dead security guards and one highly damaged assassin.

Morrigan was waiting when they crossed through the portal into the abbey's landing chamber. "Did you find anything that looked like a poison, or an antidote?" she asked, anxious.

Ruby feigned a scowl. "We're fine, thanks for asking. Are you perhaps referring to these?" She held up two small, matching vials that she'd found on their fallen foe. One was empty, and the other was filled with what looked like lemonade and glitter.

Her sister abruptly snatched them from her hand and took off at a run.

Ruby and Idryll followed at a more reasonable pace and caught up with Morrigan as she came out of a room, closing the door behind her. "The parents were poisoned with something. The healer thinks you might have brought the antidote."

"Are they in danger?" asked Ruby.

Morrigan shrugged, a little worried. "Not out of the woods, but if that's the right potion, everything should be fine."

"The kid?"

She chuckled. "Wanted to go back and help kick the bad guy's ass."

Idryll grinned. "Good start."

Ruby stretched and sighed. "There's nothing we can do to help right now?" Her sister shook her head. "Okay. Then let's go find Abbot Thomas. I need a beer in the *worst* way."

CHAPTER TWENTY-NINE

Margrave sighed as he moved the oversized cat prowling his worktable away from the item he was examining, *again*. Ruby laughed. "Come on now. You know you love her."

He shook his head. "No, I don't think I do."

Her laughter increased. "Give her time. She'll win your heart."

He frowned while poking at the collar of the magical armor set with a pair of tiny probes. "What kind of a name is Idryll for a cat, anyway? What's wrong with Fluffy, or Noodles, or maybe Dust, given her colors?" The feline hissed at the insult, causing Margrave to join in Ruby's mirth. He clarified, "Okay, not Dust. She *is* magnificent. I'm still not quite sure why she's here, though."

That was a legitimate question but difficult to explain. In part, Ruby had brought her along because she felt a little rocky after the fight, both mentally and physically, and needed the stability of having her partner around. She'd had nightmares about getting shot, about how close she'd come to dying. They all ended with her cursing herself for being arrogant, or naïve, or perhaps some of each. Fortunately, she'd survived to learn that vital lesson, and the bad dreams were lessening in intensity and frequency, to the point where she could almost hope that one day she'd be able to sleep through the night again. Physically, she felt weird although the magical potion had healed all her wounds. She couldn't think of another way to express it other than *off*. If she had to place a bet, she'd go with it being the start of a deeply annoying cold.

She shrugged. "She's my service animal. Anxiety, at the moment." Another hiss from Idryll expressed her opinion on that matter.

Margrave nodded. "Whatever makes you happy, crazy person. Now, where did you say you got these?"

"From someone who won't need them anymore." He shot her a look, and she shook her head. "Sorry, you're not getting any more than that."

He tapped on the table with one of the probes, making a rhythmic *clicking* sound that communicated his annoyance. "It wouldn't have anything to do with the fracas at the Kraken, would it?"

Ruby smiled. "I can neither confirm nor deny that."

"Maybe you know something about the cat people or the archer everyone's talking about?"

"Neither confirm nor deny."

He heaved another sigh and pointed one of the probes at her face. "Remember our deal. You have an obligation to stay alive and healthy so you can test my stuff."

She nodded. "No worries on that front. I'm doing all I can, believe me."

He turned back to the items on the table. "Well, this

stuff is pretty interesting, but I'm afraid it's not going to be useful again anytime soon. You see here and here?" He pointed at where two missing chunks of metal ruined the etchings. She nodded. "Without filling these perfectly and a flawless fix on the etchings, it would be entirely unsafe to wear."

She growled, "Dammit."

He laughed and replied, "Careful with the salty language there, sailor."

Ruby scowled. "This would've been an awfully handy tool for someone to have."

"A cat person?"

"I don't know. What do you think, Idryll?"

The cat gave a dismissive meow and sat primly, staring at them both. Margrave observed, "I've never seen such a condescending look on an animal's face before."

Ruby replied, "Right? She's something." Suddenly, her vision blurred and she grabbed the edge of the table as a wave of pain and sickness shot through her.

Margrave, startled, jumped up to steady her. "Red, are you okay? You just became a unique shade of pale green."

Ruby shook her head, which turned out to be a bad idea as the pain increased. "I don't think I am."

"I'll call an ambulance."

She grabbed his wrist. "No. It's apparently time to reveal a couple of secrets to you. First, that cat isn't a cat." The *venamisha* magic did nothing to stop the declaration as it traveled from her brain to her mouth.

Idryll jumped off the table and transformed into her humanoid form. She took Ruby in her arms, easily lifting her with one arm under her thighs and the other under her shoulders.

Margrave's jaw hung open, but no words came out. Ruby's head lolled a little as she confessed, "Second, I'm not human." She let the illusion hiding her heritage drop and waved an arm, summoning a portal that opened to Keshalla's house on Oriceran, a connection the woman had instructed was for emergencies only. *Dying is probably an emergency, right?*

Sounds came through a long tunnel to reach her ears as Margrave asked, "You'll take care of her?"

Idryll replied, "On my life, always." Her partner stepped through to the other planet, and Ruby let the portal collapse.

She asked, "What's going on? Am I dying?"

Idryll shook her head as she carried Ruby into Keshalla's bedroom and laid her down on the bed. "No, you're not dying. You're being *called.*"

Memories of the *venamisha* crashed down on her, but that pain had been nothing compared to what she felt at the moment. She hoped it wasn't an indication that whatever challenge awaited her would be proportionately worse.

Ruby managed to force out only three words before she tumbled into the blackness of unconsciousness. "Again? Bloody hell."

Ruby has made new allies and faced new challenges, but those challenges haven't ended. Her destiny still awaits her in *A FLUSH OF DIAMONDS.*

Book three in the series is A Flush of Diamonds, and it's available now at Amazon and through Kindle Unlimited.

Thank you for reading Book 2 in the Magic City Chronicles, and for continuing on to read these author notes! I hope you enjoyed the tale, especially the involvement of the Federal Agents of Magic!

This book was hard to write. Like, really hard. Usually when I'm writing there's a pivot point where it feels like the uphill climb turns into the downhill spring, and the story just rolls out. In this case, I didn't get there until the second chapter in the Kraken, which is far later than usual.

I'm not overthinking the reason; as always, I'm just grateful that it all came together in the end like it was supposed to do. I love the way Morrigan progressed in this book, really enjoyed the parts with Diana, Rath, Glam, and Deacon, and made myself laugh out loud a few times at the things that came out of Idryll's mouth.

In writing communities there's a lot of talk about whether you're a "plotter," or a "pantser," the latter meaning that you just write by the seat of your pants, making it up as you go along. Stephen King is a great example of the latter group, as he's said before he just thinks of people in a situation and goes from there. I tend toward the former, since my books tend to have a lot of moving parts. Ultimately though, I think it's a blend – I make a plan, and then the characters mess up that plan, and then I make a new plan.

For instance, the second part of the venamisha wasn't supposed to happen until book 4, but apparently it's coming earlier. While that makes the road a little rocky and requires some solid rethinking of things, it's also what makes the process so exciting for me as an author. I find turning points that I never expected and treat them as gifts.

Another example is that I had planned to give Ruby the magical armor she took from the assassin. But I realized that gave me the Superman problem – if your protagonist is too powerful, what threat is there, really? So it's broken, at least for now. But I wouldn't be shocked to see it coming back again soon.

World of Warcraft was a bust, but it only cost me $15 to avoid spending a couple hundred on a game that no one was going to play with me, so I count that as a win. I finished Avengers, but haven't done the first DLC yet. I'm playing Cyberpunk 2077, but I'm really, REALLY disappointed. The glitches aren't so much of an issue as the storytelling. Coming from the game studio that did the Witcher 3, this game just doesn't come close to what they're capable of. Such a deep set of ideas to work with, and they've just rehashed a ton of stuff we've seen before.

The holiday season always means new board games for us. The thing I'm most looking forward to is Sherlock Holmes: Consulting Detective, which we're going to play as a family. I'm a huge fan of mysteries in general and Holmes in particular, so I think it'll be fantastic.

The Expanse is every bit as amazing as it promised to be. I'm not sure there's ever been any sci-fi as good as this show on the small screen. Watching season 2 of the Mandalorian, but seriously, the first episode is Raylan Givens in space. I loved Justified with a deep and abiding passion, but for heaven's sake, at least change the accent a little. The darn thing is even called "The Marshal." Come on people. Work with me here.

The holidays are always a weird time for me. The lack of structure is a challenge. I'm one of those people that just wants to rest while I'm working but can't relax when there are things left to do. It's a devious little catch-22.

I've been rereading the entire "Foreigner" sequence by C.J. Cherryh to keep my brain from obsessing about things I can't control. It's a really lush, wonderful tale. Slow, rich, and vibrant. I can't think of another series that has those qualities that I enjoy even half as much. I highly recommend it to you if you're a fan of science fiction.

Finally, if this is your first taste of my Urban Fantasy, look for "Magic Ops." I promise you'll enjoy it, and you'll get more of Diana, Rath, and company. You might also enjoy my science fiction work. All my writing is filled with action, snark, and villains who think they're heroes. Drop by www.trcameron.com and take a look!

Until next time, Joys upon joys to you and yours – so may it be.

PS: If you'd like to chat with me, here's the place. I check in daily or more: https://www.facebook.com/

AuthorTRCameron. Often I put up interesting and/or silly content there, as well. For more info on my books, and to join my reader's group, please visit www.trcameron.com.

.

230

.

In my never-ending quest to get healthy, stay healthy I'm trying something new. Instead of taking one more exercise class with someone yelling about just one more while I wonder if planks count as some kind of torture - I've ditched everything that I don't like.

This is the radical advice of my trainer, Laura Weiner, who I've known for years. (The thing I like about her the most is when I ask a question, sometimes she says, *I don't know*, and goes off to research a thorough answer. Rare and wonderful.)

And, instead of looking for ways to exercise, we've been looking for fun things to do that involve movement. Stay with me here. This was weirdly mind blowing.

Laura's direction was to ditch everything I approached as a chore and look for things I'd actually look forward to doing. This conveniently fits in with my quest to regain the optimism, curiosity and joy I had as a kid. You know, that feeling when you wake up on a Saturday morning and realize the day is yours and your best friend is just a few houses away. I would jump on my purple Schwinn and race down the hill on Juniper Drive, wondering what adventures the day held. That wasn't exercise, even though the bike had no speeds and weighed a ton. It was the start of something fun.

I'm sixty-one years old, so it's a long way back to that little kid, but there's something strange about when you get to be this old. You let go of a lot of the have-to's and shoulds and ask yourself better questions. Like, what do I *want* to do? That question changes everything.

So far, I've found boxing and since we're still in a pandemic I've set up Quiet Punch in a doorway. It's a lot of fun punching something over and over again. The session is over before I know it and I've let off some steam.

Next up is yoga. I've been using videos from YouTube in the living room. Sure, the good dog Lois Lane usually parks herself on part of the mat, but that's just part of the ambience. Like being in a gym when a latecomer puts their mat down super close to yours. Ah, the memories of actually being in tight quarters with others. Yoga is perfect because most of the videos start with breathing and meditation and end with the same. By the time it's over I've been sweaty, I've stretched and I'm a lot calmer. Plus, there's hundreds to choose from and they all emphasize different things. I know that sounds like an ad for yoga, but it's my jam.

I tried running, which I loved but it turns out my back did not. That's another part of this experiment. I have to be willing to admit defeat with some of the ideas, let go and try again. So, running was replaced with kayaking in Lady Bird lake in January. This is Austin, which means sixty-degree weather, which to me sounds perfect. However, the rental place said, I'm the only one who's asked about lessons. Apparently, everyone else waits for the ninety-degree weather.

That meant the instructor and I were the only two boats on the lake, along with a lot of birds and turtles. It was perfect. I didn't even notice I was paddling.

Hardest part of kayaking? Getting in and out of the boat. I did some kind of weird backward entry and roll out, but it worked without entering the water. Awkward but efficient even if the twenty-something instructor, Aubrey looked confused.

What I've gotten from all of this is that moving around was never supposed to be torturous. It can actually be fun. Friends have tried trapeze lessons and hula hoop with flames. Yeah, that last one is a thing. It's all got me looking forward to what comes next instead of dreading 'exercise'. That Laura is a very clever trainer. More adventures to follow.

TR Cameron Social

Website: www.trcameron.com

Facebook: https://www.
facebook.com/AuthorTRCameron

Martha Carr Social

Website: http://www.marthacarr.com

Facebook: https://www.facebook.com/
groups/MarthaCarrFans/

Michael Anderle Social

Website: http://lmbpn.com

Email List: http://lmbpn.com/email/

Social Media:

https://www.facebook.com/LMBPNPublishing

https://twitter.com/MichaelAnderle

https://www.instagram.com/lmbpn_publishing/

https://www.bookbub.com/authors/michael-anderle